It's About Time

Published by Mission Point Press
2554 Chandler Rd.
Traverse City, MI 49696
(231) 421-9513
www.MissionPointPress.com

ISBN: 978-1-950659-57-9

Library of Congress Control Number: 2020938375

Printed in the United States of America

It's About Time

Anne Edmondson Barbour

Mission Point Press

One

"*I*'m getting tired of this."

Talking to herself as she often did, Austen Wiley groaned as she hung up the phone. She had just agreed to deliver a proof copy of CompuMart's new magazine promotion when its office closed. That made the third time this week for such a request, and once again it would be past eight o'clock before she could pick up David since the trip to CompuMart and back would take at least two hours.

Later, as she drove her car out of the underground parking, she began to wonder, not for the first time, if success was worth it. It had taken some lean years to convince the upper echelon in the advertising agency where she worked to consider her for print production. Even in these enlightened days, they still seemed to view women only in the lowest level entry positions. Oh, she had spent her time in clerical positions, and appreciated all they did in keeping everything running smoothly. But as a single mother, Austen had wanted the opportunity to earn more. She couldn't deny that her present position of print production manager fulfilled that need.

Now, after those first few years, she was doing okay. But it was taking a toll. Doing well meant working more than the normal eight-hour day, and it wasn't unusual to spend entire weekends traveling back and forth to printers for press checks. Added to all that, there had been mention recently of adding TV and internet ads to her responsibilities, which would mean more training and perhaps even conferences out of town, leading to more time away. It seemed that advancement for her came at the cost of less time with her son. And lately Austen had noticed he was depending more and more on his thumb for security. The habit that had once been so endearing was incongruous now. David was only four years old, but tall for his age and no longer a baby.

Hours later, she picked up the section of newspaper lying beside her recliner. With her son settled in bed with his much loved cuddly bear, Austen finally had a chance to relax. Dressed in her favorite old soft jeans and Kansas University sweatshirt, she snuggled down into the comfort of the old chair with a cup of chocolate-flavored coffee. Almost unconsciously she opened the paper to the page where she had circled: "Summer Employment, Memorial Day-Labor Day. For the person who Loves History, Likes Outdoors, not afraid of hard work. Would consider family. Reply Box 140K."

She kept staring at the ad. It was not so common these days to advertise for employees in the newspaper; but this outfit was not nearby, and maybe they chose this method to reach a wider readership. It gave no hint, other than "likes outdoors" of what the job would entail. But for the last several weeks, she had turned to the help-wanted section of the Sunday newspaper, her eyes drawn to this page, this ad. That phrase "would consider family" seemed to leap out as if beckoning to her. It's only for the summer, she thought, but if I could have David with me…

I must be crazy, she thought, rising from the chair. I'm finally doing a good job of supporting David and me and here I am considering giving it up. What would I do when fall comes, me with no job and David ready to start pre-school? It's probably just spring fever, and I'll get over it.

Nevertheless, she went to her antique writing desk, rummaging through its slots for pen and paper. She ran her hand over the glowing finish and traced the intricate carving with her finger, remembering the day she and Don had spied the piece, dirty and falling apart at an outdoor flea market. They had spent a summer of weekends scraping, gluing, sanding and polishing to get it to its present state. They had intended eventually to furnish their home with antiques, but that dream had ended with his death. Brushing aside her memories, Austen quickly jotted down a reply to the ad. She could type up her response at work.

In the following days, David seemed to become more clinging, not wanting to be left at day care and reverting to babyish ways. And things didn't change at work. Austen was kept so busy that she almost forgot about her response to the ad. A client called with a question about billing, though she had carefully gone over it before it was sent out. Materials were late for another project, and she spent more time than she would have liked getting the necessary extension from the publication it was to go in. In between she was putting together a production schedule, and it was beginning to look like she might have to personally check on a four-color job being printed out of town.

So she wasn't quite prepared when she picked up her mail a week later. Quickly going through it, she stared at one envelope, almost afraid to open it. It had come. Well, she thought, it's now or never. She tore open the envelope and pulled out the letter. She had the job, "if I want it," she whispered, then laughed. "Boy, do I! I think."

Three weeks later, Austen could tell that her mother was wondering about her sanity. Austen had been surprised when she received such a quick reply to her letter, and somewhat amused to learn that the position was with an outfit that, among other things, provided wagon treks that followed one of the old trails.

Well—so much for that, she had thought, and set it aside. But when CompuMart complained for the third time in one day about some minor change in their ad, Austen decided success wasn't worth the hassle and turned in her resignation.

She notified her landlady, giving notice on her apartment, made arrangements to store her furniture for the summer, and nervously stopped by to see her parents. Austen needed to let them know about this somewhat major adjustment in her life. But she also wanted to ask if she and David could stay with them a few days before they headed toward the northwest.

She watched her mother look around the room at the antiques and Oriental rugs. During the last few years her parents had slowly replaced the worn carpet and battered furniture which had filled the house when Austen and her sister, Linda, were growing up. It took no imagination to know that Donna Morgan was wondering if those things could withstand even a few days of a little boy's exuberance, but she guessed too that it was a delaying tactic. The woman needed time to absorb her daughter's disquieting news. Austen had always been the quiet, steady, practical daughter, not given to such impulsive actions.

Instinctively sensing her mother's apprehension and concern, Austen touched her on the shoulder, then impulsively hugged her.

"Look, Mom, I know you think this is crazy; maybe I do too. But I'm a mother too, remember? And I'm tired of never seeing my son, of having others spend more time with him than I do. It would have been different if Don hadn't been killed, but he was, and David shouldn't have to do without both parents."

She wondered if she was trying to convince her mother or herself. Several times in the last couple of days, she had almost panicked thinking of her uncertain future. She had gone through that once before after her husband's death and had vowed at the time to never be in such a precarious position again.

"Oh, honey, your life hasn't been easy these past few years, and I ache for you." Mrs. Morgan released herself from the hug, stepping back. "But a wagon train? You've never much liked doing things outdoors. But aside from that, what do you plan to do when the summer is over?"

Austen gave her mother a look that said she didn't want to hear anymore—thank you—about fall and the end of summer.

Realizing she could get no further in trying to change her daughter's mind, the older woman switched tactics. "So, what's the man like who runs this outfit?"

Donna was a true romantic at heart. And if she couldn't dissuade her daughter, she was determined to search out the possibilities in the situation.

She could see the wheels turning. "Forget it, Mom. It's just going to be a summer job." Then with a shrug, she admitted, "And I don't know what he's like. I haven't met him. What little communication we've had has been by mail."

She had noticed lately that her mother was becoming less than subtle about her hints, taking every opportunity available to voice her belief that her daughter had been alone long enough. It did no good for Austen to point out that she wasn't alone; she had David.

She and Don had grown up in the same town and had been a couple since meeting at church in their teens. They married when both were twenty-two, just a week after their college graduation. Then Austen got a job and went to work, and Don had gone on to law school.

He had been an assistant to the district attorney for two years and was being groomed for politics when he lost control of his car on a wet highway and crashed into the supports of the overhead interstate. Fortunately no other car was involved, but Don had been killed. With very little insurance, it had been necessary for Austen to continue working in order to support herself and her son.

There had been a few dates in the last year. Her gray eyes set in a classic face framed by her thick blonde hair never failed to attract attention. There was no lack of men who were interested. But they also seemed to expect her to go to bed with them, almost as if they were doing a favor for a frustrated widow.

She had come to the conclusion that there was no man interested in a permanent commitment, especially when that commitment came with a child. But then, she wasn't sure she could handle the dating game anyway. Since she and Don were practically babies when they started dating, Austen wasn't sure she had ever learned the rules. And they certainly seemed to have changed since then, or maybe they had always been different for young widows. Besides, if she did have any free time, she wanted to spend it with David.

Austen came out of her introspection to see her mother's raised eyebrows and to hear, "I don't understand; surely you had an interview with someone if you got the job."

"Well, they had hired all the people they needed. Then one of the men ended up with a broken leg when he was thrown from a horse. By the time they got around to contacting me, I was the only applicant remaining who didn't already have summer employment."

Austen was grateful that before her mother could express even more anxiety, the door slammed, announcing David's arrival. His excited voice called out, "Mommie when are we going to move in with Grandma?"

A week and a half later, their car packed with enough clothes for the summer, Austen and David pulled out of her parents' driveway. Calculating that it would be at least a fifteen-hour drive, allowing for the many stops necessary when travelling with a small child, it was a very early start. But she wanted to arrive at her destination before dark.

Richard Morgan had carried a sleepy David to the car and buckled him in. The little boy was already asleep again, slumped over against the pillow propped up beside him before they were out of sight of his grandparents. Those two stood in their driveway, waving goodbye until they could no longer see the car.

Her mother had sent her off with a travel mug of hot coffee and a couple pieces of toast. She had filled up her car the night before and didn't plan to stop until David woke up. She had brought a banana to stave off his hunger in case he woke before they found a place to have breakfast.

It always surprised her how many cars were on the road in those lonely hours between midnight and daylight. Now, she occupied herself by trying to guess their destinations, wondering about their reasons for traveling through the dark. Finally, with the golden oldies on the radio as background to her thoughts, she contemplated her uncharacteristic actions of the past few weeks, hoping she hadn't made a drastic mistake.

When she told her friends at church about her summer plans, they reacted in the same way as her mother. Still, they wished her the best and prayed she would be safe in all her travels and experiences. They also promised to call. It was only after she arrived at TrailWays that she learned there would be no phones on the trail.

Their route took them almost a hundred miles north, but they had already turned to head west by the time David woke up. Clouds tinged with purple, pink, gray, and blue signaled the rising of the sun. A glance in her rearview mirror showed her the reflected burst of orange light appearing just before the first round rim of the sun appeared.

They made steady progress across Nebraska, with the Golden Arches becoming their modern-day guideposts. David seemed to be ready for a stop every time they came into view. Once, after visiting the restroom, he came out with a puzzled look on his face. "Mommie, did the wagon train peoples have bafrooms?"

"No, honey, they didn't."

"Well, what did they do when they had to go?"

The place was crowded, but David's little-boy voice still attracted the amused attention of several nearby people waiting to give their meal orders.

She thought to herself that it wasn't getting any easier being a single parent. But there seemed to be unique problems when that single parent was a mother and her child was a boy.

He had asked a simple question, and there was a simple answer. Austen explained as best she could and just hoped he understood. The little boy had never been camping, so didn't have any experience with outdoor facilities. Judging from the look on David's face, though, it would take him no time to become accustomed to that kind of situation.

All during her explanation, she kept thinking Don should be here telling his son about such things. But then, if Don were still alive, she and their son would not be in a car headed toward the panhandle of Nebraska for some job she knew nothing about. And she wondered again about that job. Would they be outdoors a lot? And would she become accustomed to it?

As they continued on their way, Austen wished she had more time to enjoy the wildflowers which were just beginning to bloom in the median and beside the road. In their season, there would be goldenrod, milkweed, and prairie roses, and others with names like ironweed and compass plant. The shooting star with its pale pink swept-back petals might later blanket the slopes. Some of the early pioneers had described this area as "rolling prairies … decorated with a growth of flowers so gorgeous…as to exceed description."

In the fields along the interstate, shoots of corn or some other crop grew in regimented rows; windmills turned in the breeze, the wooden frame of one of them patched with dozens of crisscross pieces of wood to hold it upright. There too were the pivot sprinklers, looking like some kind of giant insects, spraying the field as they turned in slow circles. It seemed that the present day occupants of the land had no need to depend on the foibles of nature as the early-day settlers did.

Still, today, their route followed the Platte River. Described in those pioneer days as a mile wide and a foot deep, too thick to drink and too thin to plow, it held peril in its currents and quicksand for those crossing it. But now, Austen knew much of it was being diverted by dams, and the loss of the wetlands was adding to the endangerment of some bird species.

If their trip had been a month or two earlier they might have seen the sandhill cranes as they migrated. The Platte had been an important stopover for the birds for about ten million years, according to what she had read. After wintering in Mexico or Texas, the cranes gather for their flights toward Canada and Alaska and their breeding grounds. The channels of open water on the Platte also attract lots of other water fowl, as well as the bald eagle which nests along the river. She thought she would like to be here sometime when people from all over the world come to the Platte Valley to witness the congress of birds, especially the 'cranes of the grey wind'. Eighty percent of the world's sandhills are here during the spring migrations.

David laughed when she told him about the cranes' distinctive dance.

"Well, it may be just to relieve tension, but it caused the pioneers to call them preacher birds, since it looked as if they were leading their flock in joyous prayer."

As they drove along, Austen thought of all the different kinds of people who had traveled along this way back in the 1840s: farmers looking for new land; storekeepers who hoped to set up new shops; carpenters, missionaries, teachers, all the occupations of the day. She wondered how she would have fit in. Maybe she would have been a teacher wanting to try something new, anxious and apprehensive, but excited as she embarked on the adventure toward her future. Those men and women were no cautious stay-at-home types. They held the hopes and dreams for a better life, and were willing to take the risks to achieve them. Well, perhaps she wasn't so different; that could certainly describe her present situation.

It was close to sunset when they turned off the main road where a covered wagon advertised TrailWays. Driving another mile down a country road, then a long driveway where old battered boots graced the tops of the fenceposts, Austen drew to a stop. Tired, but relieved they had reached their destination. Austen knocked on the door of the closest building, introducing herself to the woman who answered.

"You're Austen Wiley?"

At Austen's nod, the woman burst into a spasm of chuckles.

Puzzled at the woman's reaction, she asked, "Is something wrong?"

"No, honey; nothing, absolutely nothing." Sticking out her hand to grasp that of the younger woman's, she introduced herself. "I'm Katherine Pearson, housekeeper at Trail-Ways. People call me Kate."

She could hardly wait to share with her husband the news that Mark's newest hand was female. No doubt about it, he was probably going to be incensed. Still, Kate thought how God sometimes worked in mysterious ways, and this was going to be a good thing for the man, whether he realized it or not.

Mark had taken over from his parents five years ago, when they decided to retire and move to a climate where the weather didn't change so drastically from season to season. She and Bill had worked for them and had known Mark since he was a boy. Though they were about the same age as his parents, they had no interest in leaving the state, so continued to work for him.

The two had watched the last few years as single women flocked around Mark, but he had shown no interest in a serious relationship, perhaps because none of them challenged him in any way. In fact, it seemed they went out of their way not to do so. In her first meeting with Austen, Kate believed this young lady was going to be different—independent with a hint of fragility about her. How she wished she could be there when Mark met her for the first time.

Looking down at the small boy standing next to Austen, she said, "You must be David," then delighted him by shaking his hand too.

"Now, I know you have to be tired after that long trip, but let's get your car unloaded so you can get settled. Then if we find you need anything else before going on the trail, we can pick it up in Plattsford."

Austen knew she had been expected; she had their letter offering her the job, and she had sent a reply letting them know when she and David would arrive. There had been plenty of time to arrange their lodging. But despite her warm greeting, Kate suddenly seemed unsure what to do with them after they took their suitcases out of the car.

Mumbling something about it not being proper to put them in the bunkhouse, she led them back into the house.

"Just drop your luggage here." She pointed to a corner of the roomy kitchen. "We'll take care of it after you talk with Mark. He'll have to let us know where he wants you."

Sometime later when she presented herself at the door of the house which served as headquarters for TrailWays, she recalled Kate's earlier words about going on the trail. She probably should have taken time to learn more about the specifics of this job she had accepted.

The man who came to the door was not exactly welcoming. His well-worn blue jeans were faded almost white in some areas, and the red plaid flannel shirt he was wearing was half-buttoned, as if he were in the process of getting dressed, or undressed. Austen wondered where that thought had come from. Even in his stocking feet, he still stood several inches above Austen's five feet six inches. A stubble of dark beard shadowed his chin and drew her attention. It was in stark contrast to the thick silver of his hair and what she could see of his youngish face. The long lashes surrounding his hazel eyes were also dark. Tanned skin stretched over his square face. Lips which might have been full and sensual were pursed together as she made her survey.

A warm flush stole over her cheeks when her gray eyes met his. It had been a long time since any man had elicited such attention from her, and she cursed the blush that was betraying her.

He looked down the path she had just traversed, as if looking for someone else before asking, "Who are you? Kate said she was sending our new hand down."

His husky, raspy voice sent shivers down her spine. And as Austen stood in front of the broad-shouldered man, she had the distinct impression she was in over her head.

Two

$\mathcal{W}$ell, Austen whispered to herself, it's too late to change my mind. Then she spoke up to admit, "I'm it—er—she."

"You're Austin Wiley?"

Disbelief or maybe it was scorn that filled his voice as the man turned back to her. She could almost feel the glare. Her makeup had long since worn off and she was unaware that her bare face, unruly hair and tired gray eyes gave her a fragile, vulnerable look.

With his eyes continuing to measure her, he said, "I need a man for this job. That's what I thought I was getting. You knew that."

Unconsciously her stubborn determination manifested itself with clamped teeth and a raised chin. So this is Mark Thomas. So much for making a good first impression. She laughed at the thought of her mother's romantic notions. But then, he didn't exactly fit the description of the man she had expected either: someone in his fifties, someone more staid and beginning to go to flab, not this man with his dash of sensual arrogance.

Austen replied in the same aggressive tone: "How would I know that? Besides, what difference does it make? Your ad said it would be ideal for someone who loves history and likes the outdoors. I fit both of those requirements."

She hoped he didn't notice her crossed fingers. Of course she liked the outdoors, going on picnics in the summer, swimming, even going on a two or three mile hike once in a while. In her reply she had mentioned doing some camping. But that had been fifteen years before when she had been a girl scout. And she hadn't exactly enjoyed it.

History, though, had always fascinated her. As soon as she learned the job involved the Oregon Trail, Austen had gone to the library to learn more about that time when people gathered in wagon trains to head west. Her thoughts drifted back to the day she and David had made a special trip to visit the National Frontier Trails Center. She remembered the little boy's excitement as he watched a handful of living-history enthusiasts in the camp they had set up outside the Center. Even their children were dressed in period clothes, as campers, traders, or Indians. David had wanted some clothes just like theirs and asked his mother if they would be living in tents when they got to Nebraska. She had bought him a hat and it had hardly been off his head since. He even took it to bed with him.

Mark's voice broke into her memories. "That may be true. But with a name like Austin, it didn't occur to me I was communicating with a woman."

The way he said "woman" almost made it sound like a dirty word.

"Then you should have paid more attention. You would have noticed that my name is spelled with an 'e.' And obviously, I'm not a man. If you wanted a man, you should have specified that in your ad!"

"It still comes down to the fact that you've made the trip for nothing, however your name is spelled. I'm sorry about that, but I don't hire women for the trail. And now, I've got to spend time I don't have trying to find another hand."

Austen's heart sank as he turned away and started to close the door. But she wasn't giving up that easily, and without thinking, grabbed Mark's arm, then quickly dropped it as he turned back.

"You, you obstinate chauvinistic man!" She couldn't think of enough adjectives to describe her feelings. "What do you have against women? Don't you know there are rules against discrimination? I guess it doesn't matter to you that I drove fifteen hours to get here. My little boy is tired and hungry, never mind me. But then, you probably wouldn't care about that. You probably really didn't want a family either!"

For a moment Austen thought she saw a sad, vulnerable look cross his face. Then she turned away, not wanting him to see that she was close to tears as she thought about the drastic impulse that had compelled her decision to come here. The coldhearted man would certainly not want to bother with an emotional woman. And she was still determined to find a way to get him to change his mind.

Almost to herself she said, "I've got to find someplace to spend the night, anyway. I'm too exhausted to think about anything else right now."

She refused to think about telling David. He would be so disappointed if they couldn't stay. She thought about the little boy's imaginings as they had made their way across Nebraska. Power lines marched through the sand hills and rough ravines. Windmills and beehives dotted the countryside, but it was easy to envision those days in the past when Indians roamed freely and emigrants with their wagons struggled to reach their next night's stopover. David was more than ready to pretend that he was one of those hardy pioneers, or perhaps an Indian scouting out their progress.

And now, if she couldn't find some way to make Mr. Mark (misogynist) Thomas change his mind, they weren't going to have the summer to spend together. She would have to start immediately looking for another job. Possibly she could go back to the advertising agency, but it was not really a road she wanted to go down again. One consolation for her son, though, was they would have to stay with her parents for a while until she had earned several paychecks. He would enjoy the time with his grandparents.

She should have listened to her mother. Of course, if Mrs. Morgan were here, she would no doubt encourage Austen to use her feminine charm to persuade Mark to change his mind. The thought actually created wild fantasies, but considering her experiences with him so far, she was convinced that any charms she might have wouldn't work on him.

She stole a look to find the man's eyes fixed on her, then quickly averted her face. It was a good thing he couldn't read her mind. There was an aggressive sensuality about him, and she felt a tug of attraction, disturbingly primitive. A frisson of electricity had raced up her arm earlier when she had impulsively grabbed his. She could easily visualize this man leading a wagon train into Indian Territory, or at the front of a cavalry charge.

She felt a hand on her shoulder and turned to look up into Mark's eyes. Surely that couldn't be sympathy she saw there.

"Look, I'm not that hard a person. It's about time for our regular Friday Night Feed. You and your boy can eat with us, and you can spend the night in one of the cabins if you're not too particular. They're pretty primitive, with few of the amenities of even the cheapest motels. Or you can drive back to Plattsford---"

She had phoned her mother when they got to TrailWays to let her know they had arrived safely. That was before she had met the bulldozer known as Mark Thomas. And before her future had become even more uncertain. She wondered what she could say to her when she made the follow-up call she had promised.

Mark's hand was still on her shoulder, and she was sure he could feel the pounding of her heart. She really didn't want to take any charity from him. But she was too weary to drive back anywhere, so she accepted his offer. They had passed the log cabins as they drove in, and David had asked with excited anticipation if that was where they were going to live. At least he would have one night's adventure.

They retrieved their luggage from Kate's kitchen and had barely got their suitcases inside the cabin door when the clang, clang of the triangle that served as the dinner bell sounded.

A shower would have felt good; Kate had showed her the arrangement in the attached lean-to. But she went instead to a corner of the room where a red and white checked skirted table held a blue granite wash bowl, a bucket of water, and a dipper. Fluffy white towels and washcloths were stacked on a shelf underneath. She dipped some water into the wash bowl, then reached for the soap and a washcloth. For now, she and David would make do with what her grandmother referred to as a "spit bath".

The TrailWays cookouts were well-known and regularly drew crowds of tourists and people from the nearby farms and towns. On this night there was the usual cowboy fare—ribeye steak, baked potato, and all that went with it—along with one of their specialties, sourdough bread. For the last thirty minutes or so, a steady procession of vehicles, clouds of dust trailing behind, had come down the long driveway.

Cars, pickups, and van loads of people pulled into the parking lot that was nothing more than packed-down dirt, but hard as concrete after years of such use. Their cabin stood at the edge of the parking area, so Austen and David were able to follow some of the latest arrivals toward the haze of smoke and food smells.

A wagon pulled by two black mules and just returning from one of the two-hour trail rides drew to a stop. Its passengers dislodged near a group of cars and wagons that were circled as if to ward off an attack by Indians. Some people were on the path that followed the course of the Platte River which flowed close by. She and David stopped to watch a couple of the night's guests playing a game of horseshoes. It was a peaceful setting, quiet, relaxed and far from the city's hustle-bustle pressure. Austen felt encompassed by a feeling of total serenity. It would be so good to lose herself in this, if only she had the chance.

The appealing aroma of sizzling steaks wafted up from the two big specially-made grills. Several people had already filled their plates and were seated where rows of tables and benches were arranged under a covered area.

She recognized Kate and headed toward her. The house-keeper was in animated conversation with a man whose back was to Austen. When she got within earshot she heard, "—you should have told me when you called that she was a woman! You know I don't hire women for the trail!"

Kate started chuckling as she looked past him and he turned to see the object of his aggravation. He sent a glare in Kate's direction, then returned his attention to Austen. The quick splash of cold water and her cursory washup had done a lot to revive Austen, making her feel somewhat better able to face the man. She had brushed her hair smooth and pulled it back, then tied it with one of the red bandannas presented to her by her father when he learned about her summer job.

As Mark watched her approach, his anger seemed to fade, only to be replaced with some other emotion. For a moment, their eyes caught, fascinated, searching, question-ing. A strange electricity flickered along her nerves. Then Mark pulled his eyes away to look down at the child holding tightly to Austen's hand. David had stayed with Kate while she confronted Mark, so this was his first sight of the little boy. He ruffled David's hair as he crouched down to the boy's level.

"Who are you, cowboy?"

"I'm not a cowboy; I'm David Wiley." Then his thumb popped into his mouth.

"Glad to meet you, David Wiley. I'm Mark Thomas. And you must be pretty hungry if you've got to chew on that thumb. Why don't you come with me, and we'll fix you up with some food."

David couldn't take his eyes off the man, gazing adoringly at the tall man in his cowboy hat and boots, tight jeans, and western shirt. With a big grin, he trustingly put his hand into Mark's.

Mark tipped his hat to Kate and Austen, said, "Ladies," then, leading the little boy, headed toward the stack of plates waiting to be filled.

Austen couldn't believe it as she stared after them. Mark had been so mean to her; how dared he try to charm her son. Kate soon disappeared too, leaving her to fend for herself. She was hungry as she hadn't eaten much at any of the stops they had made. She filled a plate, then found a place at one of the tables. It didn't take long for her to find that everyone was friendly, not like the irritating owner of the place. But she avoided saying much about herself, letting them think that she, too, was one of the tourists. Besides, if Mark had his way, that's all she would be.

She caught sight of Kate several times during the evening. The housekeeper was kept busy dishing up the platter-size steaks, but when their eyes happened to meet, Kate would give her an encouraging smile. She was certainly different than her enigmatic boss. It was good to know she had a friend here, though Austen couldn't quite figure out why the woman was so obviously her ally.

Austen caught glimpses of Mark throughout the evening. One couldn't miss that silver hair, though it was topped with the hat which had so fascinated her son. Occasionally, when the crowd parted briefly, she could see there was a woman with him and David. She was almost as tall as Mark, and dressed similarly, down to the hat. The way she wore it pulled down in front shadowed her face, making it impossible to see what she looked like beyond the red hair hanging down her back. Well, it didn't make any difference to her. She was only interested because her son was with them.

But for some unknown reason, Austen did wonder about their relationship; she didn't know whether or not Mark was married, but even from this distance, she could see there was a certain rapport between the two. It was obvious to her that they were well acquainted.

It was not until time to start the sing-along around the campfire that she saw David again when Mark brought him back to her. The vexing man invited them to join in, but she declined, feeling she had done battle enough for one day. Besides, she didn't want to confuse those first minutes of their acquaintance with this softer, friendlier side of him. She couldn't afford to. She planned to confront him again the next day, and didn't intend for recollections of brazen teasing eyes to interfere as she got her thoughts together.

David was about to drop by the time they returned to the cabin, and she wasn't in much better shape. Still, tired as he was, David talked about Mark until he fell asleep. Later, as Austen laid in the dark cabin, the smell of smoke drifted in through the open window. And despite all her worries, the laughing and singing around the campfire became a lullaby, and she was soon asleep.

She woke slowly the next morning. It wasn't quite daybreak, but the rooster that lived with some hens in its pen next to the cabin had wakened her with his crow. The country's alarm clock, she thought to herself. David was still asleep in the smaller bed next to hers. As she laid in bed, she looked around at the rest of the room. She hadn't paid that much attention to it the day before.

There was a sort of loft hanging above the bed. It was reached by an attached ladder, and looked big enough for a couple of sleeping bags or a mattress. A screened opening at the peak of the roof, which was made from rough-cut oak, helped with ventilation. Bark still covered the log walls.

There were two iron beds, the double one she had used, and the single that still held a sleeping David; both were furnished with old-fashioned springs. There was a wood-burning pot-belly stove for keeping warm on cooler days, and a single electric light bulb hung over the table and the two painted kitchen chairs from the thirties or forties. A green braided rug covered the planked knotty pine floor. A shelf for holding dishes was attached to the wall above the table, and one of the boards of the attic loft was furnished with nail hooks she supposed were for holding clothes. A couple of snapshots, faded and curling at the edges, were tacked to the wall.

Reluctant to get up and not yet ready to disturb David, Austen began to put her thoughts together. How could she convince Mark he should let her stay, to at least give her a chance? Surely if there was a possibility of getting someone else, he wouldn't have hired her in the first place. A sharp knock on the cabin door startled her, interrupting her mental plans.

When the knock came again, she jumped out of bed to answer the summons. She wanted David to sleep a bit longer. She was taken aback to find the man so recently in her thoughts standing on the low stoop. She had slept in sweats and was well covered, but just the same felt shy and embarrassed as she saw the man standing there. For a time, neither said a word. Their eyes met as if searching for something. Her breath caught; she hadn't expected to see him so early this morning and wasn't prepared for how he made her feel. Unconsciously, she took measure of him. The shadow around Mark's chin indicated that he hadn't yet shaved. And those lips: suddenly she wondered how they would feel on her own.

Then her gaze reached his eyes again, and she felt she had only been fooling herself. This intractable man wasn't going to change his mind. He was probably here to see when she was leaving. As he continued to stare, she began to feel like a worm caught on a hook, squirming under his perusal.

The stoop where they were standing was small and narrow; of necessity the man and woman stood close together. The morning sun shining on Austen's hair seemed to form a halo around her face. A breeze lifted some wayward strands, blowing them across Mark's face, then curling around his finger when his hand lifted to remove them. Almost of its own volition, his other hand raised, both hands tangling into the mass, his long fingers cupping her head, tipping her face.

Almost mesmerized, Austen couldn't drag her eyes from the flashes of awareness in his eyes as they lowered to her mouth. Her heart pounded; electricity rushed through her body. Then Mark stepped back, his hands jerking away from her hair, the movement so sudden that they caught and pulled.

Austen couldn't repress the "ouch" that escaped before she looked away, embarrassed at her involuntary reaction.

He ignored the hurt puzzlement in her eyes. "That hair is going to be nothing but trouble on the trail. You should whack it off."

Her hands reached in a protective gesture to the unruly mass. Left down, it was a lot of trouble, but she'd be darned if she would cut it off to please him.

"I'll do no such thing!"

"Well, do something with it!"

"I suppose your wife has her hair cut short in one of those boy cuts to satisfy you!"

She watched him stomp off. He hadn't bothered to respond to her statement. She didn't know why she had said it in the first place. *What does it matter to me whether or not he is married?* she thought.

Then she recalled what he had said. Turning to go back into the cabin, she consoled herself. Maybe there wouldn't have to be any convincing arguments after all.

But she still wondered exactly what he meant by "on the trail." Somehow it sounded different than all the other times she had heard it.

A short time later, there was another knock. With a noticeable twinkle in his eye, the man who stood at the door told her, "Kate sent me down to invite you and your boy to breakfast."

Extending his hand, he introduced himself. "I'm Bill and it's a pleasure to meet you. I usually just tell people I belong to Kate. Guess we sort of belong to each other, we've been married so long."

Austen soon learned that like Kate, Bill was a fixture around the place. She had to smile to herself when she realized that he readily fit the description of what she had thought the owner of this place would look like, though there was certainly no flab about him. He was as sturdy as the bluffs in the surrounding vicinity.

She guessed correctly that the reason Mark had come to the cabin earlier was to invite her to breakfast. "Don't know what happened to him," Bill told her. "Mark's usually so calm, he's dull. But he sure was perturbed about something." Bill gave her a look as if he knew exactly what that something was. "Guess he forgot."

Austen recalled those moments when, for just a moment, she had thought Mark was going to kiss her; and she would have let him! Strange, that was not like her at all. After years of avoiding any kind of relationship with the opposite sex, to have been so close to falling into the arms of a man she had just met. And one she didn't particularly like at that—and one who obviously didn't like her.

Apparently everyone else had already eaten, because it was just the two of them and Kate in the comfortable kitchen, where the housekeeper fed David and Austen flapjacks, bacon, and eggs.

"You know, this is pretty much what breakfast is on the trail," Kate told them, "though sometimes you might have sourdough biscuits."

Turning to David, the woman asked, "How did you sleep, young man?"

The little boy still seemed awed by everything. It was an exciting adventure for her son, and Austen was still trying to decide how to tell him they might not be staying. There was an aura about the place that wrenched at something inside her too. A feeling of anticipation she couldn't quite put a finger on, as well as a strong sense of history that she wanted to explore.

She wasn't paying much attention to what Kate was saying to David until he said, "Boy, Mommie, I get to feed the horses and the chickens! Kate says I can prob'ly pet the baby horse too. Did you know they call that big horse that lives by our cabin the grandma horse? Kate says she's real old, but she had a baby. Do you think Grandma Morgan might have a baby?"

Austen wondered what she had missed. She had seen the horse and colt in the pasture next to the cabin where they had spent the night. The old mare seemed not much more than skin and bones, though she was very possessive of the feisty young animal.

She looked questioningly to Kate as she automatically answered her son. "No, David, horses and people are different."

The housekeeper seemed reluctant to let her in on what was going on, instead informing her, "Mark wants you to meet him down by the wagons when you finish your breakfast."

At Austen's raised eyebrows, Kate, seeming even more reluctant, went on, "You'll need a jacket, and be sure to wear sturdy boots or shoes." Then, almost grimacing, the older woman added, "And he said to do something with your hair."

Her first inclination was to pay no attention to the orders Mark had left for Kate to relay, but she wisely suppressed that notion, knowing it would do nothing to help her cause. She stopped back by the cabin where she and David had slept the night before and rummaged through her luggage for the jean jacket she had packed, then took just enough time to twist her hair into some semblance of a bun. She knew the mass would soon slip out of the pins holding it, but never mind, she had done something with it.

The imperial owner of the place was busily loading items into one of the small covered wagons when she arrived. What looked like duffel bags went into the body. Mark placed cooking pots and utensils in a partitioned box-like contraption attached to the back, then added foodstuffs, and even an ice chest. She could see that the box was already filled with staples, and guessed he must be preparing for a trek.

"It's about time you got here."

Mark looked her up and down as if to satisfy himself that she had carried out his instructions. "Where's your hat?"

"Kate didn't say anything about a hat. Besides, I don't have one."

"Well, you've got to have a hat."

Grumbling something under his breath, Mark walked the short distance to a small building and came out carrying one made of straw, which he shoved onto her head. The hat wasn't new and she wondered whose it was. It could even be his; it would take a bigger size to cover the mass of hair piled on top of her head.

He then led a pair of black mules toward the front of the vehicle. She stared at the animals almost fearfully.

With one of his infuriating grins, Mark introduced her: "Meet Jack and Jennie, two of our most important workers. Today they're going to pull the wagon out to our encampment. As you can see, I've already packed the things we'll need, but there'll be other times when you will be responsible."

She acknowledged his words with a slight nod, not trusting her voice enough to try to speak, her heart was hammering so. It seemed to have leapt into her throat. He was going to give her a chance!

Then, unable to keep the excitement out of her voice, Austen looked around before asking, "Where's everybody else?"

"There is nobody else. It's just you and me, Mrs. Wiley. Our first customers will be here in two days and you've got a lot to learn. But we'll have to make do with a crash course."

She saw his mouth tighten, his lips clamped disdainfully together. There was power and an aggressive sensuality about his face, a look that almost dared her to protest.

"Okay, first lesson."

At that he proceeded to direct her as they harnessed the mules and hitched them to the wagon, with Mark naming each harness part as they went through the procedure—bridle, bit, blinds, hames, collar, trees, and more.

"Do you expect me to remember all that?"

"It's part of the job, so yes, you need to learn the name of each part and its function." Mark gave her a challenging look.

Always the job. She heard the impatience in his voice. What a summer it was going to be. But she admitted to herself that in one way it wasn't that much different than her job in the advertising and print world. There, too, she had to know how each part of the process fit with the next to create the best finished product.

"But for now, the main thing you need to remember is the lines," Mark told her, pushing them into her hand.

When she had finally gotten the team hooked up to the wagon, he ordered her up to the seat, then climbed up beside her. Making sure Austen had a good grip on the leather reins, Mark called, "Wagons Ho!" and the mules started forward.

She wasn't prepared for the unexpected jerk, and momentarily lost her balance, falling against Mark. He had stretched his arm across the back of the seat and now brought it around her, his hand cupping her shoulder to steady her.

"You okay?"

Surely she imagined that gentle concern. But for a moment, Austen relaxed into the unexpected comfort, experiencing a sense of warmth and peacefulness along with an unexplained sensation of yearning.

Not wanting to misinterpret his actions, she might have been too brusque in her assurance that she was fine. She felt a definite sense of loss when Mark withdrew his arm, then turned to face forward as if to ensure there would be no more accidental contact. Thinking back on this later, Austen thought it was just as well one couldn't predict the future.

Three

Several weeks had passed since that day. She gave the stew another stir, then stepped back, careful to keep her long skirt away from the blazing fire. Its charred hem already testified to previous close encounters. Her sweaty fingers combed through stray wisps of blonde hair. She had piled the thick mass into a loose knot on top of her head, but it was still intent on escaping the restraints of her bonnet.

The rest of the wagons were pulling up and circling, preparing for the night's stop. David was in the lead one, and she could see him happily smiling at the wagon master who was riding alongside. Watching him, she thought back to the day she and her son had gone to Independence to visit the place where many of the emigrant trains started out. When the two had visited the National Frontier Trails Center, they had seen artifacts which had been found along the famous route. Now, David hoped every day to find a treasure himself, and she didn't discourage him, though she was sure everything had long since been picked up.

At least her son got along with the austere man. She hadn't succeeded in pleasing Mark Thomas yet. Weeks spent more on the trail than off, and, at least in his eyes, she was still inept at practically everything.

As for herself, thinking it would help her prepare for the job, she had read up on the historical trail. In an antique shop, she had even found a book written by a man who had traveled the trail in the 1840s, the same period of time that the wagon trains had been crossing these expanses. She had gotten into the habit of creating fanciful tales based on those events, to the delight of David who was always ready for "just one more." Mark was also impressed by her talent when he overheard one of her imaginative creations. Her storytelling had since become a regular part of the entertainment, and now all else began to fade as she looked toward Chimney Rock, which loomed nearby. It was perhaps the most famous landmark of the Oregon Trail. As she gazed at the spire, the next tale began to take shape in her mind.

"The Willis family had left Independence, Missouri at the end of March in their wagon, which was one of twenty-five. They had sold nearly everything they had to afford the trip, making sure to pack their Bible, tools, and clothes, along with everything else they thought would be important. They would have liked to take other things, but had learned that people on earlier trains had needed to discard items.

They had heard of Chimney Rock which was about five hundred mile from Independence and were anxious to ---"

Her thoughts were soon interrupted by David, who ran up to her, laughing, "I told Mark that riding in the wagon made me all shaky inside. He sayed that's how a milkshake feels."

Automatically she corrected, "Mr. Thomas."

"He sayed I could call him Mark. All the other bodies do."

Austen sighed; everyone except her. She hadn't yet been granted that privilege. Probably never would, at the rate she was going. More than once in these last few weeks she had told herself she might have been a bit hasty in leaving her secure job in advertising.

There, she had begun to be recognized for her unique ability to handle difficult projects. And she was always the one called for when a particularly precise eye-to-detail was needed. But here in the wide-open spaces, it was a different story.

She remembered that first day out on one of the week-long treks, when, tired as she was, she still had to prepare the evening meal. She had re-dug the pit to the precise directions Mark had given on that trial run—one foot wide, one foot deep, and three feet long, with each end sloping forty-five degrees. He had told her that his research revealed those dimensions allowed for the most efficient cooking. Of course, on that memorable day, the mulish man had made her dig a fresh pit. Only afterwards did she learn from Bill that the participants on the treks were given the privilege of doing all the tasks, and that often the same fire pit was used over and over, just being filled in after each use.

When she had challenged Mark with that knowledge, he gave her a pointed look, then told her, "Look, my men have to know how to do everything, and why."

He had then proceeded to remind Austen, "The people who come out here pay good money to experience life as it was. They expect expert, authentic instruction, and I aim to see that everyone gets it. It's especially important for those who come for the graduate course."

At her blank look, he asked, "Haven't you read any of our brochures?"

"If you remember correctly, Mr. Thomas, I wasn't hired until late." Her chin came up, and with hands on hips, Austen had dared him to comment. "Since then, you've kept me busy from before dawn until after dusk. By the time I finish all my chores at the end of the day, all I want to do is fall into bed. I've hardly had time to do any extracurricular reading. I didn't know I was expected to be a professor too!"

She had turned from him, so missed the slight lifting of his lips and the amused light in his eyes. "Don't worry, you don't have to be; the college sends its own. We just provide the living history."

❧

Now Austen smiled at her earlier incompetence. Thank goodness she was doing somewhat better at building fires since that first trek. The intrepid Mr. Thomas would have taken care of it that first day out; and she probably should have let him. Especially when after she had removed the dirt from the pit, added the firewood, and correctly placed the iron bars and grate, she still couldn't get the fire started. But as usual, her stubborn spirit had refused to admit defeat.

It hadn't helped her temper any when Mark reminded her, "Well at least you didn't have to comb the prairie for buffalo chips," just before turning away to give his attention to one of the young women on the trek who had been flirting with him all day.

And things got no better. When she had finally managed to start a blaze, it was a smoky fire. "Probably just as smoky as if I had used that prairie cordwood," she muttered to herself, throwing Mark a dirty look.

The supper she cooked had at least been palatable: a nourishing stew and the required sourdough biscuits, ending with a sort of peach cobbler made from a couple of jars of the preserved fruit. And she had easily conquered the mystery of trail coffee. Just throw a handful of grounds into the big pot, fill it with water, and bring to a boil.

Though mealtime was an hour later than it should have been, everyone had taken it in good stride. Except, of course, the unappeasable Mr. Thomas. She could easily picture him, lips clamped disdainfully together, his hand rubbing across the day-old beard on his chin, his eyes fixed on her with that enigmatic expression. None of his regular employees could understand his uncharacteristic hard treatment of her. Mark was usually so easy going, allowing people to make mistakes, then stepping in to help, showing how they could do things in a better way.

Kate and Bill couldn't help being amused at the way Mark reacted to Austen from their first meeting. They loved him like a son, and kept hoping that someday, a special woman would attract his interest. It was apparent that Austen got under his skin, but at least he was finally exhibiting some feelings. In discussing the situation, Kate had said, "Well you know there's been no lack of giddy, simpering females flitting around him, and he's never given them any special attention."

At which Bill told her, "You can simper around me anytime you want."

"Oh, you," she responded, making a loving slap toward him; then they hugged. Married for more than thirty years, their love was clearly apparent.

~

It was hard for Austen to remember any soft expression in Mark's hazel eyes. Whenever he thought Austen might be weakening during her crash course, he dared her with, "Any man I hired would have to do this. Just let me know when you find it too hard."

Despite her weariness from the unaccustomed labor, Austen hadn't given in. She didn't have that stubborn streak for nothing. But then Mark brought out a tent.

"Sometimes our modern pioneers, like those early emigrants did, choose to sleep under the wagon, or in it. But they had tents too. I had these specially made; they're as close as I can figure to the ones they used. Except we had these zippers added so our customers of today can feel more secure."

With a wicked grin he added, "It helps keep out any critters that might want to share a bed with you."

She had refused to be intimidated. "You must have shown me everything by now, and it's getting late. Shouldn't we start packing things back in the wagon so we'll be ready to go back to your headquarters?"

Mark looked at her smudge-streaked cheeks and told her, "We're not going back, Mrs. Wiley. There's at least one thing you haven't experienced yet. We'll be staying the night.

That's what the tent's for, unless you'd rather sleep under the wagon."

"But we can't!"

She stared at the implacable man. He had stood with arms folded together, his back to the setting sun. And he had tipped his hat so that his face was shadowed even more, making it impossible for her to read his expression. Austen was sure, though, that he wore that infuriating amused grin.

"You didn't say anything about spending the night when you kidnapped me. Besides, there's David. He'll be expecting me."

"He won't be expecting you. He's looking forward to helping Bill with the evening chores, and then he will stay with Kate and Bill tonight."

She recalled her son's excited reference to feeding the horses, and began to wonder what else she might have missed that morning in Kate's kitchen.

"Which means you told him, a four-year-old boy, that we would be staying out here all day and all night, but didn't bother to tell me."

"Don't you think he needed to know that it would be tomorrow before his mother returned? You wouldn't want him to start worrying, would you?"

She couldn't fault the man. He may not have any children of his own, but he certainly knew how to treat them. But then, maybe he did have children. She still didn't know much about him.

His voice cut into her thoughts: "I guess I just assumed you would realize we would spend the night. It's all part of the package we offer and you have to know what to do. But if you don't think you can handle it, Mrs. Wiley, we'll pack up and go back in. I'll have wasted a day, but better to find out now."

Her eyes locked with his, Austen felt a tremor of excitement course through her body. Could she handle it? Oh yes, she could handle being out here, in the shadow of Chimney Rock for a night, but could she handle spending the night with this man? Some indefinable, long forgotten emotion gripped her when she thought about it. After these past years of being alone, why should a Nebraska rancher elicit these kinds of feelings? They couldn't even manage to get along well enough to get past referring to each other as Mr. Thomas and Mrs. Wiley.

Those feelings were reflected in her voice when she nervously admitted, "But I didn't bring anything to sleep in."

She could feel her face turning red, and hoped Mark hadn't noticed. She needed to be more careful about saying whatever popped into her head.

"You can always sleep in nothing."

When Austen glared at him, Mark told her, "Sometimes even when we go out on our longer treks, we just tell the people to pack a toothbrush and some deodorant. There're no showers, and I don't think any of them worry too much about what they're going to sleep in. They just sleep in their clothes. You can too, at least for one night. It's not as if it will be days before you can change. It'll give you a chance to experience a little of what those early pioneers did. By the time they got to Oregon, not only were they dirty, their clothes were hardly hanging together."

Since there hadn't been anything she could do about it at that point anyway, she overcame her anxiety about the coming night and made an effort to enjoy the rest of the afternoon and early evening.

For their supper, Mark had warmed up the stew that had been their noon meal and served it with slices of sourdough bread and sassafras tea. She listened to the quiet sound of his voice as he told her about some things the modern pilgrims could look forward to.

"We give each person a journal so they can record their impressions and memories. A lot of those early travelers kept diaries. That's how we learned so much about the trail. They get a kick out of the Pony Express riders coming with mail, and we give them paper and envelope so they can send a letter back home if they want to."

"Of course, one of the most popular things for a lot of folks is shooting the cap-and-ball rifle. Anyone who wants to is shown how to load it, then they pick out a target to shoot at"—noting her challenging look, he added with a grin—"inanimate, of course."

The fire had died down and the setting sun was ready to slip out of sight on the western horizon. Mark recounted some of the more interesting experiences of past years' treks. As it got later, they unconsciously settled into a quiescent silence, with Austen reluctant to disturb the unexpected tranquility by bringing up the subject of bedtime and the sleeping arrangements. She could vividly remember that earlier wicked grin, and now it seemed almost as if he were waiting for her to turn in.

I can just imagine what Mom would say about this, Austen thought, not wanting to think that her mother might even encourage her to take advantage of the situation.

It was getting cooler too. She wasn't sure she would be warm enough, even with all of her clothes on. And she still needed to visit the little tilting wooden building he had pointed out earlier when he told her, "Sagebrush doesn't offer much privacy."

It wasn't yet dark enough to need a flashlight, but Austen still had to carefully watch where she put her feet. It wouldn't do to trip. That would be further proof that she wasn't capable of contending with trail life. But because she was looking down and not forward as she returned to the wagon, she didn't realize she was so close to Mark until she fell over him.

He had been bending over, checking the tent pegs, and her tripping knocked him over too. Somehow Austen ended up on the ground with Mark on top of her, one of his legs trapped between hers, one arm curved around her shoulder, the other braced with his elbow. Her breath was momentarily knocked out of her, but she was more embarrassed than hurt. That embarrassment changed to a different kind of awareness as Austen raised her eyes to Mark's face. Composed of strong masculine lines, it was tanned and leathery from spending so much time in the sun. Unconsciously her hand rose. She fought the impulse that had her aching to raise her fingers to that dark shadow of a beard.

When her eyes rose further to meet his, she expected to see mockery. Instead, Mark's hazel eyes were almost green with a heightened awareness as they stared into the dark gray of hers. For a while they lay unmoving in this unexpectedly intimate embrace. Then, just as they had that morning—was it only hours ago?—his eyes lowered to her lips. Nervously Austen's tongue came out to moisten them. She couldn't have moved if she wanted to. And she didn't want to. She had to know how his mouth tasted, even though she knew it would be madness.

His free hand raised, his fingers traced around her face, settling around her usually stubborn chin, then tipping it up. Her eyes closed as the pads of his thumbs brushed across her full lips. He tightened his embrace and his leg seemed to settle more closely to hers. Austen could feel the throbbing of her pulse, or was it his? She wanted to wrap her arms around him, but they were trapped by the way his body rested across hers. She could hardly bear the tension, the waiting, the desire to have his lips replace the abrasive yet sensual touch of his thumbs. His knee brushed across her leg; the cloth of his jeans stretched tight. She had been cold before, but now she was burning up.

When she thought she could no longer bear the tension and was sure she would feel his mouth settle over hers, Mark muttered, "This is crazy."

He pushed himself off her, rose quickly to his feet, and disappeared into the night. She wasn't sure where he slept. They packed everything quickly the next morning and returned to headquarters earlier than planned. Their trip back was silent, except for an occasional order to the mules and the sound of the wagon wheels.

Both Kate and Bill were in the yard when they pulled in. By the glances they exchanged, it was obvious they were surprised to see Mark and Austen back so early.

David came out of their small house, rubbing the sleep out of his eyes with one hand, one thumb anchored firmly in his mouth. But by the time Austen had climbed down from the wagon, he was beside her ready to give her a hug.

"Hi, Mommie."

"Hi, sweetie, I missed you yesterday. Did you have a good time with Mr. and Mrs. Pearson?"

He didn't get a chance to answer. He looked up shyly to Mark as the man came around to where the little boy and his mother were standing. Ignoring Austen, as he had on their trip back, Mark squatted down beside the little boy.

Though David's thumb had come out of his mouth when he hugged his mother, it now popped back in.

"Say, cowboy, I haven't had breakfast yet."

At this, he darted an enigmatic look toward David's mother. "And you must not have either, if you're having to chew on that thumb again. How about we go see what we can rustle up?"

He reached out and David trustingly placed his small hand into Mark's much larger one. Then they headed off to Kate's kitchen, leaving Austen staring after them.

A little later that day, she learned that their things had been moved into Mark's house, which also served as headquarters.

"But isn't there somewhere else?" Austen asked the housekeeper. She remembered the day they arrived, when Kate had been so undecided about where to put them. "The man can't stand me, and he certainly isn't going to want me in his house."

"He's the one who ordered it done."

Austen stared unbelievingly at the older woman.

"Well, there really isn't anywhere else," Kate admitted. "We have to keep the cabins available for tourists and overnight guests. Mark had planned for you to stay in his house."

At Austen's challenging look, Kate corrected her words. "What I mean is, he expected the family he hired to stay there. It's just that none of us expected a single woman."

Noting Austen's hurt look, Kate wanted to take her in her arms and comfort her. She wondered what had happened to make Mark return so early. They must have left the campsite while it was still dark.

It was much later when she learned that there had only been a few times that a family had been hired, the last time several years before. They had expected a man and his son, and figured they could reside in the bunkhouse with the rest of the male employees. When Austen arrived with David, those plans changed, leaving Kate and Bill to quickly prepare the rooms for the two of them.

"It'll be all right," Kate tried to reassure her. "The house is plenty big. Mark's office and bedroom are in one wing. The rooms for you and David will be clear at the other side of the house. He doesn't spend much time there during the summer except to sleep. Probably the only time you'll see much of him is when you're out on the treks."

"Now since you returned early, you'll be able to go to the church service. Only a few people have arrived so far for the trek, so today it will be mostly TrailWays people."

The service was held in the same area where the Friday night meal had been served. And the same band was providing the music. There were a couple of guitars, a fiddle and tambourine, and even a cowbell. She asked Bill if they were a professional group, to which he replied, "No, just a few people who love to serve and make music. A couple of them work here occasionally; there's a teacher and a grocery store manager."

Since the next day was Memorial Day, the pastor had asked a special blessing for those who were remembering loved ones they had lost, as well as for service people, first responders, and all who would be traveling to TrailWays during the summer.

For Austen, the service brought back memories of her time with Don. She had loved him so much, but those memories seemed to be fading into the past. Still, she was grateful for the soothing sense of peace that filled her. It provided a quiet ending to the weekend that had been filled with so much upheaval.

~

And Kate was proved to be right about the housing arrangement. Mark spent little time at home. Austen wasn't sure he even slept there. It was almost as if he had gone out of his way to avoid her. But it could just be that his time was taken up with the attractive redhead she had first seen at the cookout that Friday night.

Bill told her that Lissa Courtney owned an antique store in Scottsbluff. On her buying trips, she kept an eye out for items that Mark might be able to use: books or diaries about the trail, perhaps some vintage clothing for those who wanted to dress the part. Occasionally she had even come across an article that had been picked up on the trail years before. Those were always added to Mark's collection of items that he would bring out at some point during the treks. He would explain what each was, and its use. Along with the stories Austen told, they helped to bring history alive.

She couldn't help but wonder what else the woman might provide for the enigmatic man. It was apparent they were longtime friends; but was it more than that? Kate had told her that Mark had once been married, but that the marriage had ended in divorce about five years before. He was too virile, too bold, too sensual to expect he had been celibate all that time.

Now she couldn't take her eyes off him as he helped a couple of people unharness the horses pulling their wagon and showed two others how to set up their tent. Mark even had one of them digging a brand new pit, and was explaining why certain dimensions were used. This group would be out on one of the longer treks, and after this first day would be doing a lot of their own cooking. As he went through the familiar instructions, the sound of his voice washed over her, creating a yearning that she tried to ignore. He gave her only cursory attention, and that just to be sure she could muddle through her own responsibilities.

She didn't notice when Mark glanced her way, but she heard him as he told the would-be pioneers, "As you can see, Mrs. Wiley has organized a good meal for us tonight. Pay close attention to what she's doing. Tomorrow it will be your turn."

At that she raised her head, but he had moved on to something else. Just as well, she thought. I would probably have just dumped everything into the fire. There had been such incidents, and Austen couldn't blame him much if he still wondered that he had actually allowed himself to be saddled with her for the season.

When the meal was over and the evening chores done, Mark called for everyone's attention. He had arranged a display of some of the primitive articles from his collection on a piece of canvas spread out in front of him. He challenged the group to guess the use of each piece before he told how it related to the Oregon Trail. Austen paid as much attention as anyone else to these history lessons. She hadn't been lying when she told Mark she loved the subject, and, as each day passed, she became more absorbed in the particular bit of it which involved this part of the country.

As darkness fell, Chimney Rock was illuminated by soft lights installed by Plattsford's town fathers a few years earlier. They were the only concession made to the historical significance of the place. The banks of lights positioned on the ground and pointing upward gave the landmark a natural look. But the stars were still visible, appearing so much closer than when viewed from an apartment in the city. Austen heard a howl in the distance and thought of Mark's leaving the leftovers in a spot for "that old coyote to lap up."

It was hard to believe they were only a few miles from headquarters. If it were not for the sound of semis on the highway, the rumble of trains carrying coal, or a jet flying overhead to break the spell, it was possible for guests to believe they were actually back in those pioneer days. That feeling made it easy to get absorbed in Austen's latest story.

Four

Austen looked around for David and found him on the far side of the circle with Mark and Lissa. Jealousy coursed through her, but she didn't want to examine the feeling. Was it because David had developed such a close relationship with the man, or was it the relationship Mark had with Lissa? She did feel a sense of betrayal. She could have used one of his little-boy hugs and sticky kisses. Mark must have felt her gaze because he chose that moment to glance up, his eyes locking with hers. He favored her with one of his perplexing grins before he nudged the little boy by his side and prompted David's attention to his mother. Her son gave her a wide grin and a wave. But she unconsciously returned her attention to the man by his side when she began her story.

"It was 1843, and the Wiley family had been traveling with the rest of the pioneers in their train for almost two months. They had left Independence, Missouri in May, and by now, their long days were routine. They had learned to contend with rain and mud, dust and wind, and sightings of unfamiliar animals—pronghorns, jackrabbits, prairie dogs.

Just a few days before, a herd of buffalo had passed not far from them. The huge animals had been so close that the ground seemed to shake. Each day brought something new; and though there might be danger, the excitement of the unknown touched the travelers.

Sometimes Davey Wiley and his cousin Amanda rode in the wagon to get a view from higher up, but usually they walked. They had learned early that an hour of walking amounted to about two miles of ground covered. But when they rode in the wagon, they felt every bump as it went through the ruts left by earlier travelers.

The wagons moved slowly, traveling only ten or fifteen miles in one day, fewer if there were problems. If there was a river to cross, it could take days for all the wagons to get to the other side. At one of those rivers, there had been some Indians with a raft. The two cousins had been frightened, but the wagon captain had given the red men some beads and a little money so they would ferry the wagons to the other side.

The captain told the emigrants that they would probably encounter Indians from several different tribes—Blackfoot, Cheyenne, Sioux, Dakota—but they were mostly curious, usually friendly, and just interested in trading for something they wanted. Some of the things that interested them were cloth, red paint, and glass beads. And the pioneers all wanted moccasins. The captain also told them that when an Indian gave a gift, he expected something of equal or more value in return, and if he didn't receive such, he would reclaim the gift he had given.

Indians rarely attacked the emigrants on the prairie, though they might beg, borrow, or steal anything they could get their hands on. The cattle and horses were special targets, which led to the wagons being circled at night to form a corral for the animals to keep them from wandering off. Then the men took turns with guard duty. A job of some of the older children was to sit on the backs of the wagons during the day to keep an eye out for any wily red man who might have caught sight of the train.

The party had negotiated Ash Hollow a few weeks before, an area where the road was rough, with hardly a level foot anywhere. And the final descent there was so steep that ropes had to be tied to the wagons, and the wheels locked to get them down. But that marked only about a third of their trip, and the roughest part was still ahead. Still, it was a welcome relief, for water, wood, and grass were available.

Along the way, they had seen carved oak bureaus, shattered wrecks of claw-footed tables, and chairs that had been thrown out by people in previous wagon trains. Those cherished relics of ancestral prosperity in colonial times, perhaps originally imported from England, carried across the Alleghenies to remote Ohio or Kentucky, then to Illinois or Missouri, had been left behind to lighten the wagon load. Amanda had cried when she saw a dresser just like the one she had in her room back home.

But there was a different kind of excitement about the camp one particular morning. As usual, it was still dark when the pioneers started stirring. Someone had to start a fire so they could cook breakfast. And just like every other day, there was a lot to do before they could get in line with the rest of the wagons in order to be on their way by seven o'clock.

Davey's and Amanda's anticipation seemed to urge them on, because by the time they had stopped the night before, Chimney Rock was visible.

It was a landmark they had heard about and now it loomed on the horizon, a spire reaching seven hundred feet toward the sky. Earlier travelers had described it, painted it, climbed it, and scraped their names into it. They wondered what caused it and wrote that the chimney was crumbling away and disappearing fast. The cousins were anxious to reach it and have a chance to climb it while it was still standing.

But then their parents told them that on a clear day it could be seen for a distance of forty miles and it would be another three days before they reached its base."

At the end of her narration, Austen pointed toward the Rock, "As you can see, it hasn't crumbled away, though it's reported that a large piece fell in 1927, and a lightning bolt stripped seventeen feet off about forty years ago. Some even speculate that the army used it for battery practice before that. It's now a National Historical Site, and still today inspires awe in those who pass its way, appearing from the distance like a needle pointing toward heaven. The peak still stands three hundred seventy five feet above its base, and five hundred feet above the Platte River.

And just as it was a monument for those early settlers, you could say it was a monument for the Indians too, those little 'one-feather' Indians. Because one sits on top of Chimney Rock wrapped in his blanket with his hands folded and under his chin, facing the setting sun, maybe saying an Indian prayer. And if you look really closely you might see the headband that holds his feather on, perhaps see a tear come out of his eyes for those lost days and times."

Austen was unaware that Mark could hardly take his eyes off her, only occasionally checking to see the crowd's reaction to her recitation. Her face would become animated, just as if she had been with those early emigrants. She knew history; that was apparent, and the visitors always enjoyed her stories.

Still, he resented Bill's telling him, "Mark, you need to think about that angle from now on. Of course, you probably should just plan to hire that young lady every year. She tells those stories better than anybody ever has."

When Mark gave him a stormy look, Bill chuckled and added, "Yeah, better than you too. Of course, whoever has done the telling before mostly stuck to the dry facts and didn't embroider any fictional family into it. But then again, she makes it all fit with the facts. And giving names to the people makes it more personal."

"Yeah, it's too bad she can't do other things as well. It's a wonder we still have anyone coming for the treks. I'm surprised her ineptness with the meals hasn't gotten around by now. Maybe people don't really expect any better on the trail." Mark shook his head, a wry grin on his face, then turned to see Austen looking at him as if he had struck her.

Their eyes held as Bill added, "Sure, they pay their money for this outdoor experience, but who's to say what the food's supposed to taste like."

He hadn't noted her presence and was unaware that each word was like a nail added to her fragile ego. "Just being in this environment is kind of awe-inspiring anyway."

Mark watched Austen's face crumble, then reached toward her, but she had already turned and was quickly striding toward the wagon that had been assigned to her and David.

Seeing the consternation on Mark's face, Bill turned to see Austen climb into the wagon. "Well, looks like you've done it again, young man."

He remembered how Kate had jumped all over Mark after that first trial run when he had yelled and ranted at Austen, even asked her why she had to pick on him, telling her, "I know very well there are outfits closer to your home in Kansas. In fact, why did you even bother with the Oregon Trail? The Santa Fe Trail started in the same place."

To be sure she got the point, Mark had continued, "And Kate said you had told her there's even a major street in your hometown, just about a block from your house that is named Santa Fe—not Oregon, Santa Fe. So why are you here pestering me like some persistent mosquito?"

Bill said, "Maybe you better go apologize."

Mark threw Bill one of his "mind your own business" looks and moved as if to head toward the wagon into which Austen had just disappeared, then turned and took off in the opposite direction.

She climbed into the back of the vehicle and sat down among all the gear. Back stiff and arms wrapped around herself almost protectively, she was determined not to cry. She had thought she had grown past being so sensitive. Now after overhearing those hurtful words, she was close to tears again.

It was good David hadn't come in yet. He had never seen his mother cry as much as she had since their arrival at

TrailWays. She had always been strong, had had to be. But the stubborn determination she had arrived with had been chipped away day by day to leave this bruised spirit. If they could be seen, her emotions would probably be black and blue, they felt so battered.

It might have helped if she had known that as she chronicled this latest story, Mark had kept his eyes on her despite the attempts of Lissa and others to gain his attention. But she was absorbed in the tale, her mind drifting back to that historical time. She had glanced at David every so often. He had remained glued to the side of the man who had become his hero. Austen hadn't realized the little boy had needed the attention of a man so much. Well, at least he had chosen someone who merited his idolization. Despite the differences between her and the pertinacious man, she could find no fault with him as a person or as the object of her little boy's affection.

She was probably even jealous of the attention David and Mark paid to each other. Despite all that had occurred between her and the despotic owner of the place, she admitted to herself that she was falling in love with him; what a folly that was. Especially when he had the interest of someone like Lissa Courtney. The successful business woman seemed as at home in the outdoors as Mark, and somehow managed to remain neat as a pin, even when she rode out on the trail,; never a hair out of place.

Austen's hands reached up, pushing a wayward strand of her own wild mass back into place. She couldn't seem to affect that neatness at any time. Oh well, it was a lost cause anyway, but wouldn't her mother chuckle. Her daughter had finally become interested in a man; but what an inappropriate match, city girl and rough outdoorsman! Why they were so formal, they were still addressing each other as Mrs. Wiley and Mr. Thomas. She couldn't recall one time he had used her given name past that first meeting when he had spit it out with contempt.

Outside she heard a cough, then a rap on the wagon before a male voice asked, "Austen, you all right?"

She wasn't up to facing anyone yet, so made no answer.

"Well, I know you're in there, and I don't particularly like talking to a wagon, but if that's the way it is, I will."

She could hear Bill shuffling around as if gathering his thoughts. "I don't know how much you heard of what the boss and I were saying, and I'm sure sorry if anything I said hurt your feelings. Kate and I have really taken to you and that boy of yours. Having you around has sure sparked up the place. And I don't know what's wrong between you and Mark, but I have a feeling you missed the good part of what we were saying."

When there was still no response from her, Bill said, "Well, you just take the rest of the evening off. I'll make sure everything is secure for the night and see to David. In fact, if it's okay with you, I'll just let him sleep in the tent with me tonight; he's been wanting to do that anyway. What d'ya say?"

It was a solution for Austen, who wasn't sure she would be able to compose herself to face anyone just yet, and wasn't ready to explain her tears to her son again. So she agreed.

"Yeah, thanks, Bill. I appreciate it; tell David I'll see him in the morning."

A few minutes later, she heard the clearing of a throat, then another rap on the wagon. Thinking it was Bill who needed something for David, she drew back the sheet covering the opening, only to see Mark.

For a moment she just stared; it was somewhat disturbing to have the man this close after just admitting to herself her growing feelings for him.

"Mrs. Wiley."

How like him, standing there with his hat in his hand, acknowledging her appearance with that formal address.

"You still dressed?"

When she said nothing, he placed his hat back on his head, then his foot onto the tongue, and with a minimum of effort proceeded to climb into the wagon. He reached out to steady himself, and because she had been standing so near the opening, he landed practically in her arms.

The unexpectedness of his actions left Austen unable to move. Surely he could feel her furiously beating heart. What kind of explanation would Mr. Thomas have for that, she wondered. The darkness hid any expression she might see on his face, but she was aware of the man with every fiber of her being. He too seemed to have a problem with moving, and when he finally did, it was only to gather her closer into the sanctuary of his arms.

She should move; her head tried to tell her to, but it was overruled by her heart, which had different ideas. It was too soon after she had admitted her true feelings for the man. And though visions of him with Lissa Courtney flitted through her mind, she banished them to a dark part of her consciousness as her arms crept around Mark's neck and she raised her face up to his.

They had not been this close since that disastrous trial run, but her body still remembered the feeling of his, the length of it pressed against hers as they laid on that hard ground. Her lips almost burned with hunger for the taste of his; her tongue came out to moisten their dryness. Mark's eyes followed the path it took across her upper lip, and with a groan, he tightened his hold on her with one arm. At the same time, the fingers of one hand cupped her chin to position her mouth as he wanted it.

His eyes looked into hers as if to give her a chance to stop him; but in reply she raised herself on tiptoe in an effort to get closer. Her fingers combed through the long hair at the back of his neck, then came around to touch his face. They tingled as they brushed across the stubble on his chin, and she felt a shiver pass through her body, or was it his? Though their clothing was the only barrier, she longed to be closer.

With a mind of their own, her fingers drifted lower, to the buttons of his shirt. They seemed to have lost all ability to perform the simplest function, fumbling in their attempt. She had succeeded in freeing only one button when a small, excited voice outside caused them to jump apart.

"Mommie, Mommie, can I really sleep in the tent with Bill?"

Five

By the time David had finished his query, he was inside the wagon too. There was very little space, but Mark had managed to move as far away from her as possible. She could almost sense his discomfort and was sure he was regretting his actions of just moments ago. She did too. It was one thing to remember that other time; but now she cringed as she recalled her forwardness. If her son hadn't interrupted them, she would have had her hands inside his shirt, stroking that skin she could almost feel in her imagination.

She assured David that he could indeed stay with Bill. He could hardly contain his excitement as he quickly gathered up his bedroll and pillow. He gave his mother a goodnight kiss and was out of the wagon again without acknowledging the presence of Mark. Surely the little boy had seen him. Even though it was dark, there was no way one could miss another person in this small space.

Then she heard his little voice say to someone, "I guess Mark is going to sleep with Mommie since I'm not going to be there. So she won't be lonesome."

That was followed by Bill's unmistakable laughter, as if he had just heard a very funny joke.

Austen wanted to crawl into a hole somewhere and hide for the next few weeks. But that was what she had tried to do earlier when she had retreated to her wagon. She still stood with her back to Mark. She didn't want to look at him anyway, and was glad it was dark so she wasn't able to see what expression might be on his face. David was so friendly that by breakfast the next morning, everyone in camp would have heard his story. Hopefully they would understand that the circumstances were not as the little boy interpreted them

Gathering her courage, she started to turn around just as Mark pushed past her. Before stepping out of the wagon, he told her, "I came over her to tell you I was sorry if anything I said earlier in the evening hurt you. Now this. Well, I hope you'll be ready with explanations by morning, Mrs. Wiley."

She couldn't help herself; she curtsied with a "yes, sir, Mr. Thomas."

Then as he moved away from the wagon, she thought she heard, "Pesky mosquito!"

She woke just as the first early rays of the morning sun struck the top of Chimney Rock. Despite the events of the night before, she had fallen asleep quickly and slept soundly. Today, others would be preparing the meals. She might be called on for some advice throughout the day, but for the most part, it would provide her with a respite, a day of quietude to free her mind of restless thoughts.

"And I certainly need that," she muttered to herself. "After last night, I'd like to take myself off where I don't need to face anyone, least of all Mr. 'Captious' Thomas."

He was not around as she made her way to where preparations for the morning meal were underway. There was a lot of laughing and bantering as the pilgrims proceeded in their sometimes awkward attempts.

The man who was trying, so far unsuccessfully, to get the fire started pleaded, "Mrs. Wiley, you're the professional; show me what I'm doing wrong."

His words lifted her spirits considerably, and the morning suddenly became brighter. Someone actually believed she had some expertise, and Mark wasn't around to dispute their opinion. Even stranger was the fact that she was able to provide him with the assistance he needed, without her usual nervous ineptitude. Whether it was because she had more confidence or she didn't feel Mark was looking over her shoulder just waiting for her to make a mistake, she didn't know. But it felt almost like she was walking on air when she left to find David.

Some of her buoyancy disappeared when she learned that not only was Mark not in camp, neither were Bill and David. They had all left the same time Lissa Courtney had, while it was still dark. Mark had some things to pick up from her store, and Bill had not told Austen that he was planning to go back in to headquarters today. She guessed they hadn't wanted to disturb her this morning and since Bill had David with him, he'd taken the little boy along. They took one of the wagons, and if she knew Bill, he was letting David do the driving. She just hoped he remembered to caution David about the prairie-dog holes. The little animals were still abundant, and dug their homes like so many underground apartment houses in the area that had to be traversed between TrailWays and the encampment. She shivered as she thought about the day one of the inexperienced men had allowed a team of horses to go too fast and the wagon had almost turned over when a wheel dropped into one of the holes.

Now the day seemed to stretch in front of her, and she wasn't sure what to do to pass the hours. It might be a good time to finish reading the diary Kate had loaned her that was written by one of those courageous women who had made that arduous trek back in the 1840s. Just thinking about what those people had to endure made her thankful for each of today's small conveniences. Possibly she would come up with an idea to use in her next moonlight story time. She had been fascinated by the woman's account of being forced to abandon her china: "It was decorated with 22-karet gold and called Toledo-Delight. We buried it in a crate so after we get settled we can go back for it."

When the Pony Express Rider galloped into camp mid-morning, he had a message for her. This was to be the last day on the trail for the current group of pilgrims and since there were skilled hands still in camp, Bill wrote that he and David would be staying in at TrailWays. He didn't know what Mark's plans were regarding returning to camp; the boss had driven on to Scottsbluff with Lissa to attend an auction.

Her spirits took a plunge. Despite her nerves being always on edge when Mark was around, she realized that when he wasn't in camp, the days seemed longer. Apparently the man was purposely distancing himself from her. And not only that, but it appeared he was making an effort to reestablish a closer relationship with Ms. Courtney.

Austen knew those two had more in common anyway, and she might as well admit to herself that it was time to start thinking about what she was going to do at the end of summer.

Strangely, though, the only things that came to mind pertained to TrailWays and what might be done to expand the interests of people and attract more of them to the area. She knew what they provided in the summer, but she was sure there were other types of activities that would hold diverse interest. Things like having a studio furnished with old clothes, accessories, and appropriate props where people could dress up and have authentic-looking photographs taken; walking tours to see wildflowers when they were in bloom; maybe even provide packets of seeds and instructions so people could plant their own. There could be canoe rides down the Platte; plays in winter; and special Christmas decorations.

Since her background was in advertising, she was even busily composing attractive ads in her mind that could be placed in newspapers and magazines, and perhaps even television spots. But then maybe Mark had already considered all those ideas and discarded them. She had sense enough to realize anything that was offered would need to fit in with the authenticity of the place. Maybe she should share her thoughts with Kate and Bill for their reactions before contemplating approaching the contradictory owner of the place.

Mark was nowhere in sight when the group pulled into TrailWays the next day, but Kate and Bill were there, and

David came running out to greet them. She was warmed by his young arms around her neck and his sweet kiss. But as his lips briefly met hers, she remembered that night in the wagon with Mark and wondered if she would ever feel the touch of his mouth. Then, sensing someone watching her, she raised her eyes to see the object of her thoughts. As usual, his hat was pulled down, shading his face so she had no clue to what he might be thinking.

Without thought, her tongue came out to moisten suddenly dry lips, but quickly darted out of sight when she became aware of what she was doing. Mark had pushed his hat to the back of his head and his eyes had dropped to follow the path her tongue took over the curve of her lower lip.

She felt caught in some magnetic force. There were several feet separating them, but she could not seem to move or pull her eyes from observing him. It was as if she had no control over her actions when she was around him. And that feeling had intensified since she recognized her growing love for the man. With several weeks left in the summer, she was afraid she would eventually make a fool of herself. Being in the same house together didn't make things easy, though she rarely saw him there.

Six

The professors came in mid-June for four weeks. There were two women in their mid-forties, and a young man in his thirties—Jonathan Smart. They came a few days before the students in order to learn more about the treks prior to the time they would all participate in the hands-on experience, expecting it all to become part of their lessons. This included the preparations made before actually starting on the trail. When they heard of the stories Austen occasionally recounted, they believed they would mesh beautifully with their presentations. Students who had applied for the class would come within the next few days. The overall plan was to give them an opportunity for college credit.

It hadn't taken long for Jonathan to notice Austen, and he was especially impressed with her stories. Almost everyone observed that wherever she was, he found some way to be close to her. She was unaware of his attention, probably because she was always so conscious of Mark's presence. And Mark was among those cognizant of Jonathan's extra attention toward Austen, as were Bill and Kate, who were amused at Mark's trying to ignore it.

Mark believed he was successful in staying away from Austen after Jonathan arrived, but the older couple saw that he couldn't seem to keep his eyes off her and was always searching for her when she wasn't in plain sight. She didn't notice that either, since she went out of her way to avoid him.

A square dance rarely occurred at TrailWays, but two weeks after the college faculty and students arrived, one was held. Several people who were in a square-dancing club in town had decided to experience the trail themselves. They had talked to Bill, who convinced Mark to make arrangements for one.

As soon as Jonathan heard about the dance, he cornered Austen to ask her to be his partner. She would have preferred not to, but square dancing seemed fun, and who else would there be? She had actually learned a little about the dance many years ago when she was a girl scout. She would be rusty but should be able to pick up on it quickly. She even remembered some of the calls, though probably not the movements that went with them—Allemande Left, Do Si Do, Promenade, and several more, even in the most basic square.

The area where they often held church was used for the event—tables were pushed back, and chairs arranged as a seating area for those choosing not to dance. A stage was erected for the band, and the organizers made sure to reserve sufficient space for the dancers. Electric lights illuminated the area, but a few gasoline lanterns were hung too, giving an appearance of an old-fashioned barn dance. Since there were no bales of hay, there would be no concern about igniting a fire.

The caller for the square-dance club visited everyone in order to gather enough couples to form one or more squares. He took time to give some basic instruction to those taking part, most of whom had never even seen a square dance. When he felt they had learned enough and a good crowd of observers had taken up most of the chairs, he signaled for the band to start the music.

David was seated with one of the families there for the trek, and waved to catch his mother's attention. She made note of where he was sitting so she could quickly find him at evening's end.

She hadn't expected Mark to participate, but there he was with Lissa as his partner. Obstinately he made sure he was in the same square she was in. Kate and Bill were also ready to dance. The same western band that had played before provided the music. One of their regular gigs was playing for the square dances in town.

She had not anticipated any of the tension she seemed to always have when Mark was around, especially since he was not her partner, and there wouldn't be any touching. She was wrong.

During the dance there were times when doing the Right and Left Grand, and when they changed partners, she found herself in his arms for brief moments. So she continued to be more aware of Mark than of Jonathan, who had no clue of the connection between Austen and the other man. He had welcomed this innocent opportunity to hold her for brief moments.

It was a relief at the end of the evening when she could gather up David and go home. But they had barely gotten in the door when Mark arrived. Even though they were living in his house, they weren't usually in the same room at the same time.

Kate had been right several weeks ago when she said that they would hardly see each other. But tonight he had come so quickly after her and David, she wondered if he had followed her on purpose.

His first words were, "So where's the professor? I thought maybe he would have come home with you."

She gave him a pointed look. "Why would that be? We were only dance partners tonight—nothing else."

"You seemed to enjoy it enough."

"I did—what about Lissa?"

They had been standing feet apart, but at her words, he moved closer into her space.

"What about Lissa?"

She looked around for David and saw that he had climbed up onto the couch and fallen asleep, so he wasn't available to help dispel the tension.

"You seem to be with her a lot."

"Does that bother you?"

Before she could answer he continued with, "The professor has followed you around ever since he got here. I doubt he's done any teaching."

As far as his question went, she knew she could say, "Yes, it bothers me," but past that, could she give any reason? Though she and Mark seemed to have some strange connection, it wasn't one in which they actually shared feelings. In fact, practically any words they exchanged seemed to be filled with contention.

Why was it so hard for them to have a regular conversation? If she didn't have something to defend, she felt like a lovesick school girl too shy to speak to the object of her affection. Especially since she was sure he didn't feel the same way—though she hadn't yet figured out the reason for some of his actions or reactions.

After a few moments, still ignoring any explanation about Lissa, he brushed past her, picked up her sleeping son, and said, "Let's get him to bed."

When they reached her part of the house, she looked around, hoping she had left everything in order. A few toys were lying there, along with a crossword puzzle book which Mark picked up, leafed through, then gave her a smile. Maybe that was something they had in common.

"You want to put him in pajamas, or not?"

"No, he can just sleep in his clothes." As she said that, she recalled that first rehearsal night on the trail when Mark had told her she could sleep in her clothes, and looked up to see his eyes on her as if he too were remembering.

When she reached to take off his shoes, Mark's hands were there already. She jerked back as if she had been shocked, then left him to finish the job and lay David down, covering him with the sheet.

As soon as that was finished, he turned without saying anything else and headed toward his section of the house. When she heard a door close, she was unable to tell if it was to his rooms, or maybe even the one leading outside.

It was only later that she contemplated Mark's comment about the professor and wondered about it. Did he think she had encouraged Jonathan? And if it bothered him, why?

That night she dreamed about Don, which hadn't happened for a long time. In the dream, they were visiting with a man they had just met. When he turned her way, he seemed familiar, with silver hair topped by a western hat. He reached out to shake Don's hand, smiling at her, then the dream ended.

The next morning, she was trying to interpret the dream when David asked if Mark was still there. He had no memory of being put to bed, and was sad that he hadn't spent the night. She wondered if maybe she should have made an effort to keep him from caring so much for Mark. What would happen when they had to leave and go back home?

Several weeks of the summer still remained, so she had some time to consider that part of her future. Her parents had expressed an interest in visiting to spend a day or two with her and David. She had talked to Bill—leaving Mark out of the plans—who had made sure there would be a cabin for them when they arrived for the July Fourth events.

In none of her texts or calls to her mother or her friends had Austen mentioned the strange, strained relationship with the enigmatic owner of TrailWays. She had hardly said anything about him, only giving them information about what happened on the treks, letting them believe he was much like her imaginative description before meeting him. But she had told them how much David liked him.

Since her parents would be there within a few days, she wondered if she should say more; but what would that be? Somehow they seemed to believe he was a grandfatherly type, and were pleased about his relationship with David.

Besides, were there actually words to describe the electrifying tension between them? And would it matter anyway? Mark would more than likely be friendly and solicitous, as he was with everyone else.

There were few activities planned for the next day, so Austen had asked for time off. David was growing out of his clothes and she needed or wanted a few things too. It happened to be Kate's usual shopping day, and she had invited them to go into town with her.

Mark had no good reason not to let her go, but still seemed reluctant until he looked around and saw Jonathan watching. He addressed Kate more than Austen when he said, "Don't forget to come back." What did that mean?

First things on her list were boots for both her and David, and a new hat for herself. She had continued wearing the one Mark had shoved on her head that first day, except for the days she wore dresses when a bonnet completed her outfit. She added new jeans and western-style shirts for both herself and her son.

It was still early when they finished, so Kate asked if they would like to see some of the town. Believing it would be good to learn more about the place, she agreed. Besides, it would mean being apart from Mark a bit longer.

They drove around for a while, with Kate pointing out various landmarks and stores, then parked in front of one with antiques in the window. Austen flashed a glance at Kate, who simply said, "Yes, I thought it would be a good thing. Besides, Mark asked me to take a look at a piece Lissa told him about."

She didn't quite understand what was going through Kate's mind, but, warning David about not touching anything, the three entered the store. Lissa invited them to look around, while giving a worried glance at David. No question she was concerned about having this young boy in her shop.

She was the same flawless, perfectly dressed and coiffed woman Austen had always seen, friendly, but with a condescending expression on her face. Austen couldn't help feeling awkward and inept. When Lissa led Kate to the piece she had come to see, she directed a warning look toward David.

The store reminded Austen of the plan she and Don had had for furnishing their home, and she would have liked seeing more of the antiques. Instead she said to her son, "Let's wait outside." She didn't want to spend any more time in Lissa's shop, anyway.

Kate came out a few minutes later, and they were on their way home. Home—when had she started thinking of TrailWays and Mark's house as home?

"So what about the piece? Do you think Mark will want it?"

"It's supposed to be for his house. He might have wanted it once, but not now."

Did that mean the furniture in his wing of the house was filled with antiques? The section where she and David lived was filled with nice, comfortable, but ordinary things.

Both were wearing their new clothes when they returned to TrailWays. She had left her hair down, freed from the twist that was nearly always piled on top of her head. Now only her new hat rested there, tilted much like Mark wore his.

Stepping out of the pickup, she caught Bill's eye. "Wow, look at you!" he exclaimed, then directed Mark's attention to her. "Hey, Mark, looks like we've got a new customer."

At first Mark only seemed relieved to see them back, then took a closer look. He had become so accustomed to the way she looked around the wagons, he had forgotten about that day when he first saw her. Emotions he hadn't felt for a long time, and really hadn't wanted to ever again, had risen. Still, despite his attempts to repress them, they seemed to return every time he saw her.

David broke the spell, jumping in front of Mark saying, "Look at my new clothes! Mommie sayed I am growing too fast and my old clothes don't fit. Do you like my boots?"

The man bent down beside him, telling him, "They look perfect for you. I like your new jeans too." Then he turned his gaze to Austen, whose eyes were fixed on him. Maybe the spell hadn't been broken after all.

Kate and Bill grinned at each other, then went into the house, leaving the other three standing together in the drive.

"What did you do today, Mark?" David asked his idol.

His reply surprised Austen, "Mostly I just waited for you to come home." He picked up all the packages and headed toward the house.

He seemed to be spending more time there than before the square dance, which created confusion for Austen. She hadn't decided yet whether she liked it or not. What was his reasoning? And how long would this strange truce last? She could hardly bear to be near him, and could hardly bear to be away.

She was still curious about his relationship with Lissa, but couldn't bring herself to ask Kate and Bill about it. Besides, that would reveal her feelings toward him, and she didn't want them to know. She had no idea that they were well aware of her emotions, and also those of Mark toward her. What would it take for them to figure it out themselves?

Seven

Not having any idea when her parents would arrive, Austen and David spent the day with a family on the Trail, and just as they drove in to Headquarters, saw that her parents were there. Bill had met them and was showing them to the cabin he had reserved.

They were tired and glad to be able to take a break, though it had been hours since lunch at their last stop. Bill invited them to come to the house for a meal, and, turning to David and Austen, invited them too. Remembering Austen's characterization of David's hero, the Morgans were convinced Bill must be that person.

They walked to the house, and Bill's invitation to come in had hardly been given when Mark arrived. He and Austen glanced at each other, each wondering what the other was doing there. Bill said, "Mark, these are Austen's parents; they're here for a few days," then turned to Austen, who finished the introduction.

"Mom, Dad, this is Mark Thomas—owner of TrailWays," then to Mark, "My parents, Richard and Donna Morgan."

That surprised her mother, since she had just convinced herself that Bill held that position, considering he had been the one to welcome them and get them settled.

The question of his appearance was answered when Bill told them, "Mark usually has his evening meals with us in the summer, when he's so busy with the treks."

That also explained why there didn't seem to be any meals cooked in his kitchen. Kate kept the refrigerator stocked with foods that she and David could warm up when they were there.

As soon as David had seen Mark he ran to him; and with everyone still standing in the doorway, Mark picked him up out of the crowd and was holding him throughout the introductions. David told him, "They're my grandma and grandpa."

Though he hadn't known her parents were coming, just as she suspected, he greeted them with the same friendly, responsive personality that he used with everyone besides her. Realizing he was the man who was so special to David, the Morgans gave each other a questioning look. Why hadn't their daughter been more forthcoming? They sensed there was a strain between the two, and perhaps that was the reason.

First chance he had, Mark cornered Austen to ask why she hadn't told him. Or why hadn't Bill or Kate? Now she herself wondered why. Was it because she hoped he would be away as he had been so many times, or because she didn't want her parents to see the strained tension between them?

Kate now called them all into the big country kitchen, where the table was set. Bill introduced her to the Morgans, and then she directed them to their seats, making sure Mark and Austen sat on the same side of the table, with David between them—just like a family, she thought to herself. She left it to the rest of them to find their own places.

During the meal, Mark and the Pearsons related much of the history of TrailWays. Austen hadn't heard most of it, and, listening to the words, she couldn't help thinking how the information could be adapted to activities throughout the year and inserted into her stories. Then she mentally jerked herself back to reality, remembering she was only here for a few more weeks and there had been nothing to suggest otherwise.

Returning to the present, she realized she had never been with Mark when he was immersed in a normal conversation—not one full of exasperation, as it usually was with her. Hopefully, it also meant her parents wouldn't be exposed to the usual tension between them.

Plans were made for the Morgans to participate in one of the two-hour trail rides the next day. Mark hinted that Austen might not be able to join them because of a special task he had for her, giving her one of his looks as if daring her to say anything. So much for her previous thoughts.

Her dad mentioned it had been a long day, and he was ready to return to their cabin, asking Austen if she and David wanted to ride with them. Mark interrupted, "I drove over, I'll take them home." When her parents asked where her cabin was, David spoke up: "We don't live in a cabin; we live with Mark."

There was sudden silence, except for Bill and Kate snickering under their breath. Austen could only imagine what her parents thought, and of course Mark's mouth was curved into that smug smile of his. Then without giving anyone the opportunity to say anything, he picked up David and carried him out to his pickup, with Austen trailing behind.

On their way to his house, she asked about the special job he had mentioned, to which he admitted there wasn't one. She would be able to join her family and maybe just participate in the trek instead of working. That was good, but what kind of explanation would her parents expect about her living arrangements?

The next morning, she and David walked to her parents' cabin to wait for the wagon. Since it was a shorter trek, the wagon wasn't filled with all the supplies that it would hold otherwise, so they all climbed in and found a place to sit on the floor with their backs against the sides. Rolled-up blankets softened the arrangements.

They had barely begun the trek before Jonathan came striding up, waving them down.

"Hey, we're not having classes today—can I join you?"

Austen glanced toward her parents, who nodded, and, not really having a good reason not to accept his presence, they told him, "Yes."

When he got into the wagon, he made sure to sit as close as he could to Austen, who introduced him to her parents to whom he said, "Your daughter is a really special person."

A few more feet, and they were stopped again. Mark was standing in front of the wagon and told the driver he could take the day off, because "I'm going to be in charge."

As he clambered onto the seat, he shot a look at Jonathan, who completely missed it.

Going on with his spiel, he told them, "I'm one of the professors. She's really made the summer special for me, probably knows more about the trail than I do, and I've asked Mr. Thomas to let her come help with the classes instead of work on the wagons and out on the trail. That would be a lot easier for her, but he always said no. I'm really going to miss her when I have to go back to Scottsbluff. But I may come back to visit. It's really not that far." He had no idea her time with TrailWays was only for the summer.

David had been pushed aside by Jonathan when he took his place, so Mark told him, "Come up here with me, cowboy, you can help me drive."

Everyone, especially Mark, noticed the man wasn't giving anyone else a chance to join the conversation, and finally told him, "Hey, professor, give somebody else an opportunity to say a few words. The Morgans drove a long way to see their daughter and grandson, and they need time to visit."

The word "grandson" seemed to surprise Jonathan. Had he not realized David was Austen's son? He said to Mark, "Oh, he's with you so much I thought he was yours."

At those words, his attention switched back and forth from Austen to Mark, as if wondering whether they had once been married, or was it a different kind of relationship?

His statement also convinced Mark that she had probably done nothing these few weeks to encourage the professor. Otherwise, the fact that David was her son could not have been questioned.

Then he said, "Well, they do live with me," without further explanation.

The glances Mark and Austen exchanged were actually friendly and amused, for a change; then they smiled.

At that, Jonathan said, "Just remembered a special project I asked the students to work on. Should stop by and see how they're doing."

David said "whoa" to the horses being used to pull the wagon. Hardly giving it a chance to stop, the professor climbed out and headed back toward headquarters.

Before he was out of sight, Mark said, "Not very observant for a professor. Guess he won't be following you around anymore, Mrs. Wiley."

"I never noticed, Mr. Thomas," she said, not adding that she hadn't noticed because she was always so aware of him.

Her parents wondered at the formality. Mr. and Mrs.? Was that just for this incident, or did they always address each other in that manner? Even David called him Mark.

Resuming their journey, Mark guided the horses and team to an area as close as they could get to Chimney Rock. The Morgans were impressed by its appearance up close. It would make a colorful background for pictures. He drew to a stop, arranging the wagon so it would cast a shadow to make a pleasant spot for a picnic, then unhitched and hobbled the horses.

Kate had prepared a lunch for them so there would be no need to dig a pit for cooking. Mark brought it out, along with some folding stools and an old quilt on which to arrange the food, paper plates, and tableware. Cups and a jug of lemonade which still held tiny bits of ice cubes completed the setup.

When they finished eating, the Morgans, along with their daughter and grandson, took off on a hike toward

Chimney Rock. It was impressive from afar, and they were glad to be able to see it a bit closer. A fence prevented anyone from getting too near and attempting to climb it. Even Austen was happy to have this opportunity. Since she was usually busy helping the Trail visitors, she hadn't been able to participate in the tourist thing. It was amazing how much more one could experience when someone else was in charge and taking care of all the particulars.

While they were hiking, Mark gathered up all the picnic items and stools and stowed them in the wagon, but left the quilt out. He pulled it closer to the wagon's shade, then lay down. There were few times in his busy days when he had this kind of opportunity to rest and do nothing.

Surprisingly he fell asleep, and when Austen saw him, a warm, tender feeling swept over her. It was unexpected that he would clean up the picnic, and his doing so added to this unfamiliar awareness.

Her parents and David were poking along, so she had reached the site ahead of them. She leaned down to make sure he was all right, and must have unknowingly made a small noise. Mark opened his eyes, took hold of her arms and pulled her down beside him, then wrapped her in his arms She heard him say, "pesky mosquito," before falling asleep once more.

She was trying to decide what to do when David came running up, saying, "Mommie, Mark!" then jumped on them and hugged them tightly, pressing the couple even closer together.

Mark was now wide awake, not sure what had happened; how had Austen come to be lying here in his arms? He was sure he had only been dreaming. This time he couldn't stomp off, but rose as quickly as he could, then went to unhobble the horses and hitch them to the wagon for the trip back to headquarters.

It was a quiet return trip. Austen could almost see the words whirling around in her parents' heads, and spent her time working on a logical explanation. She could tell them what actually happened, but even to her it seemed lame. Especially since she had basked in the warmth of his arms, no matter how it came to be. She had no way of knowing that similar thoughts were swirling in Mark's mind. He still didn't know how it happened, but in his heart he recognized he would have liked for the embrace, if that's what it was, to last longer.

Eight

The next day was July Fourth and Austen wondered what activities there might be. She had heard nothing about possible plans. She soon learned that there were traditions begun years ago.

It was a day of celebration, one enjoyed by the surrounding neighbors, the professors and students, as well as people from town. Red, white, and blue decorations were being hung on and around the covered stand, the houses, and even the wagons. Food would be catered by a business in town, freeing up Kate to enjoy the festivities with everyone else. The band she was now familiar with would be there to provide patriotic music all day. There would be games for all ages, and horseback rides for those so inclined, and perhaps even a wiener roast at the end of the day.

All that meant it was another day for which she had no specific duties, maybe none at all, giving her too much time to think about the happenings of the previous day. How would she react when she saw Mark; and how would he act? She knew her mother would probably track her down to ask about the day before.

She and David found her parents, or perhaps her parents found them, shortly after leaving the house. David wanted to show them around, so they all started out together. With her son along, she hoped her mother wouldn't bring up the day before. Strolling around near the hustle bustle of the area where all the preparatory work was being completed, they were soon drawn in to assisting, her dad helping set up tables and chairs, and her mom ending up helping Kate. Though she had no specific duties, she made sure there were enough paper plates and cups and tableware for the caterer's wagon. David had followed along with her dad, so Austen was left to wander around checking out all the decorations, talking to the members of the band, and discovering what was going to be available from the caterers.

Mark, also freed of his normal responsibilities, would spend the day making sure all was under control, as well as making the rounds meeting all the visitors who began arriving early in the morning. Among them was Lissa Courtney, who began searching for Mark when she first stepped out of her car. And just as Professor Jonathan had followed Austen, Lissa took every opportunity to be where Mark was. In contrast, since the day before, Austen was trying to avoid him. The same was true for Mark, who was avoiding her while trying his best to stay away from Lissa, though she didn't seem to realize it.

Even with all the people around, Lissa did manage to corner him near the catering wagon. He was polite but withdrawn, though she ignored that as she asked, "How is your little widow doing? She and her little boy were in the shop last week with Kate. Thank goodness they left the store before he could break anything. By the way, what did Kate say about that piece I told you about?"

Continuing without giving him a chance to answer, she asked, "How much longer are they going to be here? Must be irritating having the boy around." With a patronizing smile, she added, "Guess you will be a little more careful next year when you hire people. How is she getting along sleeping in a cabin?"

He could wait no longer to answer. "Maybe I'll be more aware next year when I hire people."

Austen was nearby and heard part of their conversation, but didn't wait around to hear the rest of Mark's words: "But David has been great to have around; we've become buddies. And though she required more instruction than some of my people in the past, his mom has learned well and has become a favorite with all the visitors.

"Plus, they're not in a cabin. She and David live with me. Kate didn't care much for the piece, so neither do I. By the way, you don't need to continue looking for things for me; I'll search them out myself."

With that, he turned to see Austen not far away, with what looked to be tears in her eyes. What had she heard? How much had she heard? Would there ever be a time that they understood each other, could be in the same space without misunderstanding, misinterpreting or whatever it was between them? Did it matter to her, and why did it matter to him?

Why had there been so many times recently when he made a point of telling people that Austen—and David— were living with him, as if it were some permanent arrange-ment? As if he was being possessive as well as protective.

Lissa was still standing where he had left her, a stunned look on her face. For years she had pursued the man, believing they had much in common and someday he would come to the same conclusion. He had told her that the woman and her son were living with him. What exactly did he mean by that? She knew there were different wings in his house, but maybe they were actually sharing a bed. He certainly had come to her defense. Maybe it was just a temporary occurrence and things would revert to normal when the woman left.

She decided to search out Kate to draw out her thoughts. If anyone knew the lay of the land, it was Kate. But before she could find her, Bill was standing in her path. He was too far away to hear the words, but he had seen the encounter between Mark and Lissa and guessed what had happened.

"Hello, Lissa. How are things with you?"

"Well, you know I was just talking to Mark, and I think he's been mesmerized by that young widow. I can't imagine what kind of spell she has put on him," she said laughingly.

He replied with, "Well, I don't know what might happen with those two. I just know Mark has been more alive and enjoying life than he has for years. So both Kate and I feel she is good for him. David too. He and Mark have become great pals."

With that, Lissa decided not to look for Kate after all, and without speaking to anyone else or taking part in any of the activities, she got back in her car to drive home. The widow would be gone in a few weeks, and maybe things would change with Mark.

Meanwhile, Kate had been told by Bill what had happened between Mark and Lissa, and had the feeling Austen might have overheard something that did not tell the whole story.

Donna Morgan had been in the kitchen with Kate when Bill related the incident with Mark, Lissa, and Austen. She took advantage of the circumstance to question Kate about the relationship between her daughter and the forceful owner of the place.

Kate began by relating Mark's surprise that his new hand was female, instead of the man he was expecting. That was news to Donna, since her daughter had never mentioned it. That must be why she said so little about him in her calls and texts.

"In fact, by what we had been told when we met him, we figured Bill was the owner. We were surprised by her introduction of Mark."

Kate continued, trying to explain the behavior of the two: "Even from that first day, it was clear to Bill and me that his emotions were affected, though he tried to cover it up by always challenging her. And she refused to be intimated. It's been that way the whole time she's been here. We can see that even though it's been a short time, they each have strong feelings for the other, but continue to try to suppress them. And though it's obvious to us, their efforts to do so keep them from knowing themselves."

Austen's mother then shared with her the scene from the day before, when Mark had appeared to be confused. Kate actually laughed and said, "He probably was. You say he seemed to have been sleeping? Maybe he had been dreaming and thought he still was. Knowing how he has been these past weeks, I'm sure he wouldn't purposely wrap his arms around her, especially with her family being there.

"I can assure you, Mark is a wonderful person. He's been hurt in the past, and doesn't quickly share his feelings. We've known him nearly all his life, and you couldn't find a better man. Bill and I love him like a son.

"I have to tell you, since you're her mother, that we keep hoping the time will come before the end of the season when they will admit their feelings to themselves and each other. You can't help but notice the closeness developing between him and your grandson. Not sure how either one of them would be able to survive a separation."

"Do they always call each other Mrs. Wiley and Mr. Thomas? Or is that just a put-on?"

Kate laughed and said, "Yes, if they're around each other long enough—started that first day and hasn't changed. I think it's just a defense they use to keep from revealing their true feelings."

Donna nodded, actually glad to hear all this. Having heard the conversation earlier between Bill and Kate, she asked, "But what about that Lissa woman?"

"Well, she has an antique store in Scottsbluff, and for several years has searched for items he could use for the trail. No question she would like more of a relationship, but he's never indicated any interest in such a thing."

Just then, Austen walked into the kitchen, along with David and her dad. Her parents would be leaving early the next day, and she felt they should spend some time together.

It was getting close to noon, so she suggested they go to the food wagon to get some lunch. She knew she had avoided being alone with her mother, hoping to forestall talking about what had happened the previous day, and not knowing that after talking with Kate her mother wasn't going to bring it up.

Donna later told Richard about her conversation with Kate, and they both determined to keep an eye on Mark and their daughter for the rest of their short time at TrailWays, hoping to find out for themselves what kind of connection there was between the two.

Austen and her parents spent most of the rest of the day together. David took off with Mark for some adventure. Austen learned later that they had gone for a horseback ride, getting back for the fireworks display just before dark. While everyone was oohing and aahing, David's grandparents mentioned they would like to spend a little more time with him, to which Mark suggested David spend the night with them. Austen and her parents gave him a surprised look, but David liked the idea. He remembered the night he and his mother had slept in a cabin, and wanted to do it again.

"So what are we gonna have for supper?" he asked Mark.

The caterers had left a few hours earlier, but Mark mentioned they could actually call to have something delivered from town. And when he asked what they would like, David said, "Pizza!"

He invited them to the house, saying he would call for pizza, and while they were waiting for the delivery they could have a tour, casting a look at Austen as he said it. She and David had been in the house with him for weeks and hadn't been in his section. Besides, it might relieve her parents' minds to know that they occupied opposite ends. All the while, he asked himself what did it matter, and didn't even think about the fact that if David was with his grandparents, he and Austen would be alone. Maybe he would have a chance to explain the scene with Lissa earlier in the day.

As they walked through the warm, inviting house, Austen had been thinking about it. Trying to dismiss it from her mind, she concentrated on the furnishings in his section of the house, admitting to herself it was almost exactly as she would have arranged it. The room was neat but not sterile; a pair of boots stood at attention in one corner, and a shirt hung on the doorknob of his closet. She wondered if it was the one he had worn yesterday, and why it was there. She would have liked to wrap it around herself. Looking up, she saw that Mark was watching her, and quickly averted her eyes.

Continuing with the tour, they checked out his office, where she saw that his desk was much like the one she had at home that she and Don had spent so much time to restore. And though she had hardly used the kitchen, its large country atmosphere appealed to her.

Mark gave a cursory wave toward the part of the house she and David occupied, and they all took a quick look inside without checking any further. It was not a usual practice, but doors to all sections of the house were wide open. Since the door to his rooms was usually closed, this was the first time she had seen the area where Mark spent his time.

Now he said to her, almost as if they were a couple, "Let's get out plates and silverware. Pizza should be here soon. I think there's lemonade in the refrigerator."

It was late for a supper, especially for David. His mother told him, "It's a good thing you had a chance for a nap on Kate's couch earlier today. Otherwise your head might be falling into your pizza."

Nine

When they had finished their meal, Mark drove the Morgans and David to their cabin while Austen stayed to straighten up the kitchen, all the while thinking about Mark's return and debating with herself whether to retreat to her bedroom and close the door. Being aware of the electrical tension which always seemed to encompass them, especially those times they ended up alone, she wasn't sure she wanted to deal with it tonight.

They were adults; surely they could exist in the same space without wrapping themselves in protective armor. She had run across the word "pusillanimous" in an old book. Looking it up, she learned it meant cowardly, timid. Now she thought, that was a perfect word to describe her feelings. Still, she didn't want to let her defenses down around the man, fearful of what might occur, especially when she had no idea of his feelings and was not even sure of her own.

While she was still deciding what her move would be, Mark walked in. Not giving him or herself an opportunity to say or do anything, she blurted out, "What did you say to Ms. Courtney?" Then she pressed her hands against her mouth indicating she hadn't really meant to do so.

"What do you think I said?"

"That you would be more careful about who you hired. I thought I was doing okay, but you sure didn't sound pleased about my work."

Stepping closer to her, he said, "Fact is, you please me too much. If you had stayed a bit longer, you would have figured that out.

"Now before I try to prove that to you, do you want me to put you to bed? You're dropping on your feet and I need you to be ready for work again tomorrow."

As she was picturing that possibility in her mind, she found herself in his arms, heading toward her room. He dropped her on one side of the bed, pulled the covers back, and was beginning to reach for her shirt when she stopped him.

"What do you think you're doing?" she cried out, unsure whether she was upset or not.

"Just helping," he said with that annoying grin. Then seeing the puzzled look on her face, he continued, "Don't worry, Mrs. Wiley, I'm leaving," and was gone through the door, then quietly closed it.

Before she could move, it was opened again. "I told your parents I would drive you over early in the morning so you could wave them goodbye." Then closed the door again.

While she was pondering his last words—he had first told her she needed to be ready for work again the next day, then informed her he would take her to say goodbye to her parents, the door opened again.

"By the way, Ms. Courtney won't be back, at least not while you're still here."

Then he was out the door and closing it again, this time with enough force to make her notice.

Just when she thought she had the man figured out, something like this happened. Recalling his words, she was sure she had heard him say he cared too much. What did that mean?

Mark knocked on her door at six o'clock the next morning. To her surprise she had gone to sleep quickly, although reliving the sensations she had felt when she was in his arms and being carried to bed.

"Are you up and dressed? I'm ready to go and want to leave by six-thirty."

"No, I wasn't even awake 'til you knocked, and it will take me more than thirty minutes to get dressed."

"I'll give you thirty-one."

Then she heard the clomp of his boots going toward the outside door.

At least she wouldn't have to ponder what clothes she would wear, it was pretty much the same nearly every day. She debated about taking a shower and decided she needed one. He would just have to wait.

He was standing outside her door when she opened it, looking at his watch and saying, "You're late." So much for any truce they might have had.

He helped her into the pickup and when he got in on his side, told her, "Kate is fixing some breakfast for your family, so we're stopping by there first."

Bless Kate. She hadn't even considered they would need to eat before starting out on their way home.

When they got to the cabin, Mark carried in the food; there was even a thermos of coffee. Placing it on the table, he told them, "When you finish, just stack everything together. Kate will take care of it." Catching Austen's eye, he added, "We might help," finishing with his inscrutable grin.

After their meal, David and his grandpa took another look outside. He had wanted to check on the baby horse.

Taking advantage of being alone, Donna told her daughter, "Before we leave, I would like to know more about this strange relationship you have with Mark, or Mr. Thomas, as you call him. Kate filled me in on the fact that he hadn't expected a woman, but she also mentioned that though you seem to be in constant strife, in between those times, you can't keep your eyes off each other, and she didn't think either of you were aware of it.

"The short time we've been here, I can see you care for him, though you think nobody else knows. Maybe you don't know it, or at least won't admit it. And before you say anything, I've been around him enough to see he feels the same way about you.

"And this Mrs. Wiley and Mr. Thomas, what's that?"

Austen looked at her mother and said, "Well, you're certainly not being subtle. I don't know why we continue to address each other that way. It's been going on so long I don't think either of us can change it. We can't seem to be in the same space without some kind of clash. And, you're right. I haven't wanted to experience this strong emotion that's always simmering beneath the surface. Actually, I've never really felt these kinds of emotions, even though I was married. I'm not sure anything he feels is more than temporary.

"So, yes, I go out of my way to retreat when he's near. Maybe he's doing the same thing, so we use Mr. Thomas and Mrs. Wiley to remind ourselves it's only for the summer.

"Don't know why I thought you could come for a visit and miss all this conflict. What's surprising, though it's been only a few weeks, I think I'm falling in love with him despite all the discord. He's being so good with David, and the fact that Mark is David's hero makes it hard. There have been times when he has been so tender. How will David handle it, let alone me, when we have to leave?"

Smiling at her mother, she said, "You probably didn't expect all that admission."

"I'm glad you got it out; you seem to have been thinking about it for a while. Your dad and I like him, and Kate says he's an honorable, good man—not much else to say. But don't waste time, even if you have to make the first move."

"We don't even know much about each other beyond what we do on the trail. I've seen sad feelings cross his face when certain things have been mentioned; and sometimes he has said things I don't quite understand. Kate told me he had been married and divorced a long time ago. But I don't know what happened. And, no, I haven't asked; there hasn't been a good opportunity to do so."

The two males entered the cabin then with Richard saying, "Hate to say it, but we need to get on the road."

Luggage had already been loaded in their car, so everyone gave hugs to everyone else, expressing their love, and shedding tears. Before she got in the car, Donna told her daughter, "Keep me up to date with all the happenings around here, especially with you and David and Mr. Thomas. Now that I know everything, don't hold back."

Austen and David stood waving until the car was out of sight. She felt drained after sharing her heart with her mother. And now, the resolute Mr. Thomas would have some assignment for her. She wasn't sure she would have enough energy to do it.

Remembering the breakfast things needed to be taken care of, she entered the cabin, and, puzzling David, began to cry. Apparently Mark had been keeping watch, and he appeared in the doorway, walked over to her, and wrapped his arms around her, putting her head on his shoulders, standing that way until the tears ceased. This was the first time he had deliberately done so, unless one counted the dream. It felt good, but he didn't dare let himself get used to it.

David, upset that his mommie was crying, wrapped his arms around both of them. Mark would have picked him up, but was loath to break the connection with her. For once, she had accepted the comfort of his arms without protesting. Too much energy had been spent by both of them in avoiding anything that could be construed as intimacy.

Her tears had run out, but she didn't want to move. She raised her head from his shoulder, wiped her eyes with her hands, then pulled back, looking into his eyes, trying to smile. She looked so vulnerable; he wanted to kiss her, telling himself it would only be one of comfort, but didn't dare.

Now that his mother seemed okay, David started crying. Mark picked him up, pressed him closely into his shoulder, patting him on the back and rocking back and forth to comfort him.

Austen told him, "It's not just because my parents left."

"I know."

How did he know; what did he know? She hadn't wanted to leave his arms, basking in the warmth, and not wanting to move from them. It was so comforting, and so different from their usual encounters.

"Let me take you and David home. There are enough hands to take care of the trail. Then I'll come back here to help Kate get the cabin ready for our next guest."

He set David down, then holding his hand, and with the other one wrapped protectively around Austen, they left, heading toward his pickup. When they reached the house she went directly to her bedroom and climbed into bed.

By this time, David had recovered, and since his mother was in bed, Mark told her he would take her son with him. There was a grunt from her which he took as assent.

Feeling wrung out, Austen almost immediately went to sleep. That sleep was filled with dreams of Mark and being in his arms, with no conflict or controversy between them.

Repressing a yearning to lean over and kiss her, Mark left, leaving her door open. He had managed to survive so far, living in the same house as Austen, without giving in to the longing that washed over him every time they were in close proximity.

Since he had David with him, Mark wasn't sure what he was going to do, but he needed to check on Kate. Bill was also at the cabin when they got there and there was little left to do, presenting another problem for him. He wasn't ready to return to his house yet, but needed to find something to occupy David. The couple could see Mark had something on his mind—something different—not usual with him. And why was David with him and not his mother?

"Where's your mommie" they asked the little boy.

"She's in bed."

Surprised, they asked, "Is she sick?"

"No," he told them. "She was sad when Grandma and Grandpa left, but Mark made her feel better."

Kate and Bill glanced at each other, wondering what that meant. Bill recalled the time David had thought Mark was going to sleep with her in the wagon so she wouldn't be lonely. They knew there must be a logical explanation—what the little boy saw was probably not the whole story.

Leaving it to Bill to sort out the truth, Kate asked David if he would like to help her make cookies. He had never done such a thing but thought it would be fun. As they headed toward her house, she hoped she had all the necessary ingredients.

Not giving Mark a chance to invent a story, Bill sat him down and asked what had happened.

"Nothing. Austen was sad after her parents drove out of sight, and when I came into the cabin she was crying. Without thinking I wrapped my arms around her to comfort her." After a look from Bill, he admitted, "Yes, I wanted to kiss her, but knew that would be a bad call. We usually can't be within five feet of each other without some kind of disagreement."

"When she had recovered her composure, David started crying. So, instead of having her take over one of the wagons, we went back to the house. She headed for her bedroom and climbed into bed and almost immediately went to sleep. So David and I got in the pickup and drove here."

"Well, I think that's just the beginning; there's more on your mind than just today."

And having opened the floodgates, the words came pouring out. "You're right. You know there hasn't been anyone to catch my interest since my divorce, though I do get lonely sometimes. But that first day I met Austen, despite the circumstances, I felt I had received a kick in the gut. Even though I tried to convince myself differently, I knew she was going to be here for the summer. I had no plans to pursue her, but it's been hard to stay away.

"It's been worse, knowing she's in my house. It drives me to distraction having her there; but I want her there. How crazy is that? It's a miracle if we can be together for an hour without some kind of dispute. And you've seen us; we're always trying each other's patience. But I'm dreading Labor Day, when her time here will be over. I'll miss both of them. And before you say anything, I'm sure she wouldn't want to move to Nebraska permanently—she's a city girl. So the war will continue 'til then."

Bill chuckled, "Well, that's been simmering awhile. But I think you're selling Austen short. Just look at how she has taken on all the unfamiliar responsibilities. And I haven't seen anything that would make me think she wouldn't want to stay here. If she is responding with dissension, it's in response to how you're acting."

Then Bill gave him the same advice Austen's mother had given her. "Kate and I have watched you both all summer. It's sad how you dance around each other in fear of expressing your true feelings. I heard what you said, but I also know there have been situations which would have ended differently if you hadn't been interrupted."

He ended with, "Don't wait too long; the weeks go by fast."

After the counsel from the older people, things settled down for a time; but with both of them still fighting their attraction, it was only a short time before the stormy relationship resumed.

Ten

Mark stopped by the Pearsons' to get David. He and Kate had made chocolate-chip cookies, and she sent some home with them. He told Mark it had been fun and he wanted to do it again.

When they got to the house, he stopped by Austen's room to see how she was. From all appearances she had been in bed the whole time they were gone, and was still sleeping soundly. If not for David, and if he were honest with himself, he would have climbed in beside her. So much for what he had said to Bill.

Not wanting to disturb her, Mark said to David, "Hey, cowboy, your mommie is still asleep and we don't want to wake her, but you're probably hungry; I know I am."

He checked in the refrigerator to see what could quickly be warmed up. He found a container of beef stew and asked if David liked it. He didn't remember whether he did or not,

"I like it," Mark told him, to which David said, "So do I," eliciting a laugh from Mark.

"There're some leftover biscuits here too, so we can dunk them into the stew as dumplings; is that okay with you?"

"Uh huh," the boy nodded his head. But he would have liked anything that Mark put together for a meal.

Mark dumped the stew into a pot, then placed it on the stove to warm up, stirring to keep it from sticking to the bottom. As he stirred, he looked toward the room where Austen slept, wondering if she was awake. The last few minutes he and David hadn't been as quiet as when they first came into the kitchen.

Just then, the person of his thoughts stood in the doorway, yawning and stretching and rubbing her eyes. She gave him a questioning look, and he shrugged his shoulders and grinned.

David saw her and ran to give her a hug. "Mommie, we're making stew for lunch. Do I like it?"

At that, Mark laughed out loud, then told her. "We were at Bill and Kate's for awhile, without any lunch. Found the stew in the refrigerator and some biscuits to dip in it. Want to join us?"

As she came further into the room, Mark, continuing to stir, nodded toward a chair, saying, "Take a seat." Checking to make sure the stew was warm, he turned off the burner, then put the biscuits in the microwave for a few seconds.

She chose a chair and David climbed into one beside her. He had brought over the cookies that had been sent home with them.

"I helped Kate make cookies. Want one?"

"Yes, but let's save them for dessert. We don't want to spoil our meal," Austen said, looking at Mark.

He had already set spoons on the table; next, he took bowls out of the cabinet, filled two of them with stew, and placed them in front of David and Austen. He removed the biscuits from the microwave, put them on a platter, and brought it to the table. There was milk for the boy and water for the adults.

He then filled his own bowl and sat on her other side. He picked up his spoon and started to take his first bite when David said, "I'll say grace: Thank you, God. Amen."

The two adults smiled at him, then glanced at each other like proud parents as David dipped his spoon into the bowl. After his first bite, he said, "I like stew." He ate his biscuit separately while Mark and Austen made dumplings out of theirs.

It had been a quiet meal, with David providing most of the conversation. Then Austen turned to Mark and said, "Thank you, it's delicious."

"Well, I only warmed it up. Kate made it."

"I know, but you warmed it up."

As she said those words she thought to herself, and you warm me up. How am I going to endure the rest of the days I'm here, living in the same house with you?

All turned quiet again as if they couldn't figure out how to hold a normal conversation. It had been a day when they both had poured out what was in their hearts and minds, though more than likely neither knew of the other's confessions.

Mark asked, "How are you feeling?"

She shook her head but gave no answer. She wasn't sure anyway. She still felt drained, and thought it was good she hadn't been needed on the trail. She was surprised at how long she had slept, and hoped that wouldn't affect her rest the coming night. How could she answer him; she didn't even know herself.

David broke into their thoughts with, "Can we have cookies now?"

They both seemed glad of the interruption, and took one from him as he passed them around.

"Kate said she didn't have all the stuff she needed to make cookies from scratch. What does that mean?" Without waiting for an answer, David said, "So she said we would slice and bake. She even helped me cut some of them and put them on the pan."

He started yawning shortly after passing around the cookies. Lunch had been late and it was still fairly early in the day, but it had been a long day for him with no nap.

"Hey, cowboy, looks like you're running out of gas. Maybe we need to get you ready for bed."

"I want to stay with you and Mommie."

Looking toward his part of the house where the door was open, Mark asked, "How about lying on the couch in my office to rest awhile? We can leave the door open so you would still be with us."

"Okay."

This was not a surprise to Austen; he would agree to anything that connected him with Mark.

Now Mark picked him up, and together, they took him to the room. By then he could hardly hold his eyes open. Mark laid him on the couch and removed his boots, then took a blanket from a nearby closet and covered him with it.

With that done, they returned to the kitchen, maintaining an awkward silence. Silently, yet together, they put the leftover stew into another container which then went into the refrigerator.

After putting the dishes in the dishwasher, they looked at each other as if to say, "What next?"

Mark broke into the quiet: "Guess we can work together without dispute."

Blurting out of the blue, Austen asked, "Do you have kids?"

Startled, Mark responded, "Where did that come from?"

"You're so good and patient with David, and I've noticed, also with all the kids who have been on the trail this summer. And we don't really know each other."

At those words, she noticed his imperious grin had appeared, as if he were remembering those times of almost closeness between them, when knowing each other hadn't seemed to matter.

He rose, took a seat near her, and said, "We don't have anything to do right now—maybe it's a good time to get better acquainted."

She didn't try to move; there wasn't really a place far enough away in this room where she could escape the feeling that always washed over her when he was near.

Ignoring the warm intimate sensation, she repeated her question.

"So do you have kids?"

"I'm surprised you haven't asked Kate or Bill. They pretty much know my life history."

"Maybe I will." Though she knew she wouldn't. She still hoped the time would come when they could share with each other without bringing up hurtful past experiences.

By that time, wishing she hadn't asked the question, she stood and headed toward the room where David slept. Following behind, too closely behind her, he asked where she was going; and though she couldn't see it, she knew that infuriating grin was on his face.

Without turning back toward him, she said, "I'm going to check on David."

"I thought maybe you wanted to check out my bedroom."

At that, she did turn around to confront him, only to end up in his arms; and drat her weak feelings, she wanted to raise her lips to his for a kiss—something she had longed for since that first day.

Looking into her eyes, he asked, "Is there something I should know about you?"

Thinking he already knew too much about her—about the way she responded too quickly to the least advance from him, she ignored the question. Despite the advice her mother had given, she couldn't bring herself to make the first move. Hadn't she done that by asking about children? And especially since he didn't seem to want to share his past.

She lamented the longing coursing through her body. Was it only flirting coming from Mark, or was it masking deeper feelings? Summer's end could not come quickly enough.

Where do things go from here. These hours without other responsibilities and just the two of them since David was sleeping should have given them opportunity to alleviate their differences. Instead, now there were new ones.

Maybe she needed a change of scenery to help clear her mind. Except for the day she went to Scottsbluff with Kate, she hadn't been away from TrailWays. Perhaps she should ask Mark about some specific time off. She looked toward the door that led outside, where he was standing, staring out at who knew what.

Gathering her nerve, she headed that way, then placed her hand on his back to get his attention.

He made no response, so she spoke. "Mark."

Surprised, he turned to her saying, "No Mr. Thomas?"

Dropping her hand, she said, "Okay, Mr. Thomas."

"What is it?"

Taking a deep breath, she asked, "Could I have a day off next week?"

Eyebrows raised, he asked, "Why?"

"Except for the day we went to Scottsbluff, we haven't been away from here since our arrival. I think I need a little change of pace—maybe drive to Plattsburg, or around the countryside."

Without hesitating, he told her, "Tuesday is going to be a slow day—you can have that day. I'll go with you."

Didn't he realize part of the reason, actually the main reason she wanted to get away, was to be away from him for awhile?

"Why?"

"So I can be sure you will come back."

Now she remembered those words. Why those words? What had happened to put them in his mind?

"Why wouldn't I come back?"

"I don't know—no reason to test the possibility."

Hearing those words touched her heart—there were sad things in his life—just as there were in hers.

"Okay, you can come with us. My car probably needs to be driven, so we'll take it. You can be our tour guide."

He gave no argument against the idea, so she expected that would be what happened.

Just then they heard a noise from Mark's office. David seemed to be waking up. She was surprised how much time had passed, much of it in an uncomfortable silence. It had been enough time since their meal that they began to wonder what they could eat. Maybe stew again—but looking in the refrigerator, they saw leftover pizza from the night before.

David came into the room, carrying his boots, and went straight to Mark. Seeing the pizza that had just been set on the table, he said, "Oh boy, pizza again!"

Austen was going to microwave it, but Mark convinced her that warming it in the oven would be better. It would be ready to eat in a few minutes.

Eleven

When Tuesday came, it was Mark who drove, though they did take Austen's car. It was back to Mr. Thomas, except she never noticed that he grinned every time he heard it.

They went into Plattsford, more a small town than anything else, but filled with all the stores and goods necessary for people to manage their everyday existence. Mark pointed out a couple of churches whose pastors provided services at TrailWays. They drove by a pizza shop, the one that delivered the pizza they had ordered, and an ice cream shop that David was anxious to visit.

Mark drove around for a while, just as Kate had done in Scottsbluff, pointing out the various businesses and mentioning the people who managed them, telling Austen, "If we run into them, you're going to recognize some of them."

He then pulled into a parking spot in front of the grocery store. None of the businesses were very far apart, so they could walk to any they wanted to visit. Strolling down the street, they met the young man who often served as the Pony Express Rider. Occasionally he filled in as a hand for a trek.

"This is Josh Wilson. You might remember him bringing you mail on the trail. Josh, meet Austen Wiley, an important part of our operation this summer."

She was glad to have opportunity to get better acquainted. There was an air of flirtation about him, but glancing at Mark, he chose to be more restrained toward Austen. He told her that he was a sixth-grade teacher and working on the trail had given him plenty of material for lessons throughout the school year.

Going into the grocery store, she realized that the owner was a member of the band who played guitar. His family also provided the caterer's wagon. Nearly all the individuals she met knew Mark's parents, and either they or their parents had provided service to TrailWays for many years. When the square dance caller happened to come in, he immediately began reliving the dance at TrailWays.

"That was such a good experience. I was surprised how much everyone seemed to enjoy it. You two need to come in and dance with us sometime."

Before going back to the car, they stopped at the pizza place. There was a buffet, or one could order a pizza. Mark noticed that Austen was eyeing the buffet and rightly guessed that would be her choice, so he pointed out to David how he could have samples of several kinds of pizza.

And though he was sure of her preference, he said, "Mrs. Wiley, what is your pleasure?"

Those words, "your pleasure," triggered her imagination as to what that would be and when she took a quick look at him, he was looking at her as if he knew exactly what was going through her mind. She felt a blush wash over her face, before answering with, "The buffet, Mr. Thomas." Then again that maddening grin flashed across his mouth.

It had been a pleasant day, up to now with him making an excellent tour guide, and she was just beginning to feel comfortable in his company. Then this. She hadn't discerned that slowly he was relaxing his apprehension around her and was enjoying how easily he could annoy her. But even he wasn't aware that his manner was becoming almost flirtatious.

After the lunch of pizza in all its shapes and forms, they proceeded to the ice cream shop for dessert. After checking out a few more stores, David had begun to lose his exuberant energy and the adults determined it was time to head home. She was actually glad Mark was doing the driving; it left her free to do more sightseeing. He took a different route home than the way they came so she was able to see more of Nebraska. Enough weeks had passed that some of the blooming wildflowers were different than those she saw on the way from Kansas. Since it was mid-day, no wild animals were in sight. Maybe she would see some of them—mule deer, badgers, or foxes if she stayed long enough.

David had fallen asleep before they covered very many miles. She felt herself beginning to nod, but determined to stay awake to enjoy the rare friendly atmosphere.

"Thank you for the day off."

"It was a day off for me, too. And fruitful since I was able to meet with some of the people in town. So, thank you for the suggestion."

A few more miles, and she could hold her eyes open no longer. Despite her resolve to stay awake, she too succumbed to sleep. The next thing she was aware of was Mark waking her. He had carried David into the house before coming back for her, thinking that surely she would waken and get herself out of the car.

If he were honest, it would have been his preference to carry her too. But to reach in to release the seat belt, then gather her in his arms, was basically impossible. He studied her for a time, wondering if she had any idea how she affected him. But why was that? Why couldn't he maintain an aloof response to her, as he had done with all the women he had met the last several years?

For the most part, it had been an enjoyable day with little of the argumentative attitudes they often had with each other. Could the rest of the summer continue the same way? Hopefully.

Now he squatted down beside the open door and tentatively touched her arm. His face was more or less level with hers, and when she stirred, then opened her eyes, she was looking directly into his. As if they had a mind of their own, her fingers raised to trace around his cheek before she abruptly dropped them.

"Hi," he said with not even an amused grin. "We're home." His recent thoughts had been too sober.

While David slept, the adults talked over their day. She told him she had been glad to see the town and visit with the people she had met earlier in the summer. Then she asked him if Josh was married. And before she had an opportunity to explain why she asked, he said, "Why, are you interested in him? He's probably about the same age you are. By the way, how old are you?"

"What difference does it make how old I am?"

"Just wondered if you're old enough for me." Why had he said that? He needed to be more careful about blurting out the words that were in his mind.

Ignoring his question, and not wanting to ponder it anyway, she explained that some of her friends might come for a trek. A couple of them were also teachers—one unmarried.

"I just thought they would have something in common, and he seems nice. If he's not married, I could introduce them."

"Oh, planning to be a matchmaker?"

"You're so good about taking my words and twisting them around."

With that, she almost ran to her section of the house and slammed the door, forgetting that David was there. The sound woke him and he was ready to bounce back into the perpetual motion which marked his days.

"Is Mark here?" he asked, opening the door and running to see.

Mark had left the house to drive the car back to its place in the carport, and, not seeing him, David continued to the outside door to look for him. Not realizing that Mark wasn't there, Austen made no move to follow her son, needing time to clear her head—or gather her thoughts, or whatever it would take to eliminate her unwanted reaction to that man.

When she realized she hadn't heard her son since he rushed out, she called him, with no answer. His boots were still on the floor beside his bed, so he wouldn't have gone far. It didn't take much reconnoitering—even so far as checking in Mark's rooms to determine he wasn't there. The outside door was open; would he have gone out in sock feet? Was he with Mark? If so, where? How far could he go? How long ago had he left? She didn't have any idea which way he would have gone, or which way she should go to look for him.

David had walked to the Pearsons' with his mother several times since they had been there, and, young as he was, found his way there on his own. Bill was doing some chores outside when David arrived and asked if Mark was there.

"Hey, young man, what are you doing here by yourself, and where are your boots?"

"I woked up and went to see Mark, but he was gone. Mommie was in her room, but I wanted Mark."

Not sure what to think, Bill called Mark on his cellphone, instead of Austen. "Mark, there's a little boy here who is looking for you. Could you come by to see him?"

When Mark arrived, he was surprised that the little boy was David, though he had no idea who else might have been looking for him. David ran to him, wrapping his arms around Mark's legs.

"I woked up and looked for you."

"And you couldn't put your boots on by yourself?"

"I didn't try."

Okay, where's your Mommie?"

"She's still at home."

"Did she know you were leaving?"

"No."

Just then, Mark's phone rang again, and he saw that it was Austen.

Crying, she told him, "David's gone. I've looked all around the house for him. I even looked in your rooms, then outside, but I can't find him. And his boots are still here."

It took a while for him to absorb the fact that she had called him, though he wasn't sure who else she could call—Bill and Kate?

"It's okay; he's here. He showed up at Bill and Kate's and they called me, said he was looking for me. I had left to return your car to the carport and hadn't started back yet."

"His socks are probably past saving, but he's fine. We'll both be there soon."

Why did he want to tell her he loved her as if they were parents concerned about their child? Mark, you've got to get that thought out of your mind, or head, or heart, wherever it came from, he told himself.

Before they left, Kate brought bowls of spaghetti, salad, and bread to make Texas toast. She said, "I would guess none of you will be up to putting a meal together. Hope this doesn't clash with what you had for lunch."

On the way back to the house, Mark told David, "Cowboy, your mommie has been worried about you. You should have told her you were leaving; so when we get there, how about telling her you're sorry?"

She was standing at the door when they drove up in Mark's pickup. As soon as he climbed out, David told her, "I'm sorry, Mommie."

She hugged him so closely he could barely breathe, then with tears still in her eyes, told him, "You scared me so much.

Don't ever do that again. And look at your socks! They're ruined!"

Setting him down, she continued, "I have to know where you are and where you're going. And you shouldn't ever go off by yourself."

Then without thinking, she threw her arms around Mark. "Thank you."

"Don't I deserve a kiss?" To which she kissed him on the cheek, then pulled back to put some space between them. Wrapping her arms around him had been an automatic move, but there had been the urge to kiss him with grateful relief.

Ordinarily he would have made some passing teasing remark, but not this time. "Guess that will have to do; but I would have liked something with a little more feeling.

"Kate sent supper." He had brought in the meal and set it on the table. Now the simple task of dishing it up and eating relieved some of the tension, though each was well aware of the other.

After everything was cleaned up, it was too early for bed. Mark left, saying since he had been gone, he needed to go over what was planned for the next day. But mostly it was just to separate himself from Austen. There was a television which they rarely watched, but she found a program that would hold David's interest, then picked up her crossword puzzle book to occupy her time.

Not being able to concentrate on the puzzles, she called her mother, relating some of what had happened that day, but not David's hike to look for Mark. Thinking how fast the weeks were passing, she probably needed to start preparing David for their leaving.

After talking to her mother for awhile and answering her questions about how her relationship with Mark was progressing—to which she said, "it's not"—and her mother sounding disappointed, she called one of her church friends.

Since they had once indicated an interest in visiting TrailWays, she asked if they had considered a specific time. It would be good to have reservations if they wanted to stay at a cabin.

When she ended the conversation, David was engrossed in the TV show. After his adventure, he had wanted his boots on and managed to put them on himself over his dirty socks. Shaking her head, she thought he probably would never want just shoes again.

Twelve

While he was out, Mark received an unexpected call from his brother. "Hey bro, we haven't talked for a while. How's the summer going—were you able to get enough hands? I remember you mentioned before the season began that you still needed at least one."

"Yeah, a family—well, only one child, a boy. They're staying at the house—first time for years we've had someone there."

"Oh—well, would you be able to move them to the bunkhouse for a few days? Patsy has decided she wants to go on the trail."

"Actually, no—maybe Bill and Kate could put her up—another option would be having her sleep on the couch in my office, especially if it's only for a few days. Though I know that's a few rungs down from what she's used to."

Matthew was confused and wondered why, but didn't question. "I'll ask her and get back with you. Oh, would you be able to pick her up at the airport?"

"Sure, but I need to know day and time."

"Of course, been good talking to you."

"Yeah, you too."

On his way back to the house, he tried to remember how old his niece was, maybe ten? Then he began to determine what he could do with her. He also wondered how she would get along with Austen and David; or how they would get along with her. And what was he going to tell Austen. Did it matter?

When he walked in, Austen asked out of the blue, "Have you ever been to Kansas?"

Curious as to what brought that to her mind, he answered, "Well, you might say I've been in Kansas, mostly passing through. There's never been any reason for a visit. Anyway, not long enough to decide if I like it or not, or to know much about it."

"Must be all right, though, you seem to have turned out okay. So why the question?"

"Just wondering."

Then she reminded him about the possibility of some of her friends coming to visit.

"So you said nothing about your parents being expected, but now you tell me about your friends?"

"Kate and Bill knew."

"It's okay, kind of surprised me—I thought we were closer than that," then grinned.

Sure he did, and without thinking, she grinned back.

"When will they be coming? And how many?"

"No specific plans so far; but since some are teachers, maybe the first or second week of August," thinking as she said it how soon that would be. It was already the end of July."

I don't know how many; but I would guess at least two."

"Talk to Bill about it. He's the one who takes care of the schedule."

A questioning look from her and he added, "Yes, you were correct in arranging your parents' visit through him."

"I liked them by the way."

"And they liked you." Why had she said that out loud?

"I think David does too; so that just leaves you, Mrs. Wiley."

"Now, since we're asking questions—is this so we can get better acquainted?"

"Are we?"

"Maybe. I've been wondering how you got the name Austen. And has it caused confusion for anyone before me?"

"Why did it confuse you? I think you were just so glad to get a hand, that you weren't paying attention," knowing as she said it that she may have purposely written her application letter in such a way that there wouldn't be any question.

"Perhaps not. I still want to know."

"As far as I know it never confused anyone before, so what does that say about you?"

"I'm still waiting for the answer to the source of your name. If there is one? Maybe you just made it up when you were in junior high?"

"You sure come up with some interesting theories," realizing as they continued with their banter that one might say they were having an actual conversation without an underlying argument.

His raised eyebrows indicated he would wait until she gave him an answer.

"It's my mother's maiden name. And, strangely, or not, when I was in junior high I did consider different spellings, even completely different names. I think that's not unusual for girls."

"There, that wasn't so hard, was it?"

"What is your mother's maiden name?"

"Oh, we're continuing with the name? Her name was Richards I think that's kind of interesting since your dad's name is Richard. If we ever have a son, we could name him Richard and honor both of them."

Where had that come from? He didn't dare look at Austen; didn't want to see what was on her face. Having heard the words, she didn't know what to make of it and didn't want to know if it was a serious remark, deciding the best thing was to ignore it.

As they had continued talking they had taken chairs on either side of the table and enjoyed the coffee Mark had made. Now looking around for David, they saw that he had fallen asleep while watching TV and was curled up on the couch.

In the quiet, Mark debated with himself whether to mention that his niece was coming, then decided to wait until he knew for sure. But maybe he should tell Bill and Kate, especially since he had more or less offered their place for her to stay.

"I need to get David to bed, and me too if I'm going to be ready to work tomorrow. Seems like forever since I've been on the trail." As she said it, she thought to herself, I've actually missed it, and I need to be around someone besides Mark. He would have laughed at her for not calling him Mr. Thomas, albeit in her thoughts.

He got to the couch before she did, picked David up, and said, "Lead the way. Not sure we'll be able to get his boots off."

Thinking back she remembered the times since they had been here that it was Mark who was taking him to bed, she realized it would be so easy to get used to that. If it were just her, more than likely she would have to wake her son up, meaning he would have to walk half-asleep.

They worked together in getting David's boots off. He mumbled a couple of times, but stayed asleep. Still standing by his bed, Austen bowed her head. "Thank you, Father, for David's safe return, and for those who found him and brought him home."

Even though she had a longing to continue the evening with Mark—one that was warm, pleasant, and holding a sense of tender feeling, with David in his bed, she headed for hers. Mark was still standing where he was when they removed the boy's boots, seeming to be reluctant to leave. How easy it would be to become accustomed to this family scene. Right now he didn't dare even touch Austen. She needed to get in bed, and so did he, and that bed wasn't the same one.

Finally reaching the door, he said, "It's sure been an eventful day, not at all what I would have expected at the beginning. Hope it was a good day off for you, even with David's taking off. May be the last one."

"Good night, Mrs. Wiley."

"Good night, Mr. Thomas."

For once their referring to each other in that way didn't sound like it was part of an argument.

Quietly closing the door behind him, Mark headed for his part of the house, not sure he would be able to sleep. There was too much on his mind.

Austen woke up feeling refreshed, as if she had been on an extended vacation, not spent a day with feelings ranging from apprehension to satisfaction, from panic to closeness. There had been little if any animosity, which somehow seemed to occur when she and Mark were together for any length of time. But maybe animosity wasn't the correct word; maybe it was closer to opposition. There was certainly that.

Mark's night was not so restful, having dreamed of actually staying with Austen in her bedroom, but not sure what, if anything, happened. He was dreading what the day might bring since the two of them would once again be on the trail together.

Just before leaving the house he had received a follow-up text from his brother. "Patsy still wants to visit TrailWays. Said she would be happy to stay with you, even if she does have to sleep on the couch. Looking at a week from Thursday. Let me know."

Well, that would mean another barrier between him and Austen—probably a good thing. He needed to remember to check his calendar when he was back in the house, since he would be making a trip to the airport. If she came on Thursday, she would be with them for the Friday Evening Feed, and it would also be the Sunday for church services.

To his surprise, Austen was almost animated as she hitched Jack and Jennie to the wagon she would be in charge of.

"Good morning, Mr. Thomas," she called to him as he came in sight. There was a bright smile on her face. "Are you ready for a new day?" she asked, almost as if she were the one in charge of everything.

He was thinking, "She must have slept better than I, probably no dreams to interrupt her rest."

Actually she did have dreams, but not the usual ones filled with friction. Her dreams had been peopled by a family perfectly contented in each other's company.

He stood staring at her for so long, the other hands noticed and teasingly said, "Hey, Mark, have you met our latest hand?"

Still not moving he thought, she does seem to be new and he wasn't sure he could stand to be with her without acting on his growing feelings. Then he reminded himself again that she was only going to be here for a few more weeks. Bill would have told him he could do something to change that, but he wasn't ready to do so.

He needed to check on the other wagon master and the day's activities, but instead headed toward Austen, feeling the need to be near her, even if only for a minute. He strode up to her, his back to all the people who were gathering for the trek, both workers and guests. He took hold of both her arms, and leaned down. To those standing behind him, it looked like he was kissing her, or getting ready to.

"Did you have a good night's sleep, Mrs. Wiley? I didn't; I dreamed of you all night."

She had no words for him, and had no idea how the scene appeared to the others. She had been so at ease and confident before he appeared in front of her; now she was back to her usual disquiet when he was near. And what did his words mean? They had created an intense sense of longing she didn't want to reveal.

"I had dreams."

Taking one last look into her eyes, he turned to head for the other wagon, asking himself who he was. Those actions weren't like him, and in front of so many people. Even he had no idea how it had looked to the people waiting to begin their trek.

So many were registered for the day's trail event that two wagons were needed. The group included a couple of teenage girls, bored looks on their faces. Their dads had insisted they come so they could experience something different and more important than wasting their time at the mall.

Austen was wearing jeans, her hat and boots, looking no different than the male hands, so people were surprised when they realized their wagon master was a woman and soon learned she was as capable as any of the men. That fact piqued the interest of the teenagers. Remembering the lessons she had learned on her practice trek with Mark, Austen showed her group, beginning to explain more fully the procedures followed for making a successful experience. She was glad of the return to normal to distract her from the earlier moments with Mark.

The wagons moved slowly, so many people walked, especially the younger ones, but the girls stayed as close as they could to Austen. She continued to explain steps and practices as they moved toward the space set aside for their wagon. David rode inside, poking his head out regularly to check on Mark, who was riding his horse and overseeing the entire operation.

At lunchtime, Austen directed the digging of the pit and building of the fire they would need for cooking. The teenagers were fascinated and wanted to try that chore and did a passing job. As the day progressed, they discussed applying for a job at TrailWays the next summer, and paid special attention to all Austen was doing. She didn't want to dash their dreams by telling them this was a one-time only happening, almost an accidental event.

Some had heard of Austen's stories and were disappointed they wouldn't experience that as part of their day. Hopefully next time, next year. How she wished she could look forward to next year.

As the trekkers were cleaning up the area where they had cooked and had their lunch, Austen took out a quilt and gathered the items Mark had put in her wagon to be displayed for the group. Different items were used from time to time. And just as Mark usually did, she challenged them to guess what each piece was and how it might have been used by those pioneers so many years ago. She could see that again the young girls were paying close attention and even taking pictures. She asked later if they were interested in history. They looked at each other, then admitted they hadn't been until today. Knowing she had been influential gave her a soft feeling.

While the cleanup was proceeding, Mark had come for David and they were now riding together around and among the wagons and visitors. The girls asked about David, thinking what a cute little boy he was, and, thinking they were a couple, maybe even a married couple, asked Austen about her handsome husband. Knowing they had seen the earlier scene when Mark asked about her dreams, she contemplated what her answer should be.

"No, we're not married; it's just that he and David have become close buddies this summer. David's dad died when he was only six months old."

"Oh, that's so sad!" the girls exclaimed.

Maybe their compassion would erase their remembrance of that earlier scene and their interpretation of it. With even the girls noticing the closeness between the man and the boy, she contemplated again how she would be able to tell David he wouldn't have Mark much longer.

It had been a long one-day trail event, so it was late when they all got back to headquarters. Austen and David went with Mark to the Pearsons' for an evening meal.

"Don't know if you noticed the girls with my wagon," Austen said. "Thought I should tell you they were so impressed with their experience, they've decided they want to work for TrailWays next summer."

Giving her a startled look, Mark asked, "What did you tell them?"

"Nothing. They're teenagers, and a few months can make a lot of difference at that age. But maybe you've changed your mind about having a woman?"

She was surprised he made no follow-up comment. Maybe he had changed his mind.

"Do you want to come back next year?"

This time it was she who was silent. Plus, he didn't give the impression he expected an answer. And, no, she didn't want to come back next year; she knew in her heart she still wanted to be here.

A little later she heard him telling Bill about Patsy's visit, mentioning that he had offered their place for her to stay, since Austen and David were with him. But Patsy had decided she would be okay sleeping on Mark's couch.

Bill asked, "How long is she going to be here? Haven't seen her for quite some time; she's probably changed."

"She's coming next Thursday and leaving Tuesday after that, so not a very long time. With Friday Night Feed and church on Sunday, there won't be much time to do anything else. So I hope it will be enough 'on the trail' for her. That seems to be the main reason she's coming. And I haven't seen her lately either."

Austen supposed she would be hearing more about the coming visit since Patsy would be staying at the house. Bill knew who she was. Question was, how long would it be before Mark told her? And who was she—obviously not an ex-wife or she wouldn't be sleeping on his couch. Then again, what did she know?

They had just walked into the house when she received a call from her friend Jerilyn, who told her that most of her church friends would like to visit, but with families and summer schedules that wasn't going to be possible. Besides, they expected they would see her in a few weeks when she returned home.

Jerilyn and Maggie were planning to drive, arriving on a Tuesday and leaving early Friday morning. Not long, but enough time to visit, take part in a trail event, and learn how her summer had been. Jerilyn was a teacher and believed she would be able to gather some good lesson material.

She didn't mention that they were really coming as much out of curiosity as anything else. They had heard so much from her mother about Mr. Thomas, and because she and David were living in his house, they wanted to see for themselves.

Thirteen

The next week was filled with the usual number of treks, and nothing out of the ordinary. Austen was so accustomed to the work, it was almost getting boring, giving her more time to think about the passing days, and that she would soon be leaving. Added to that, a new person would be in the house on Thursday.

He hadn't said anything about it all week, then Wednesday night Mark told her, "I have to pick up someone at the airport tomorrow. Maybe David can go with me?"

Having overheard the conversation between him and Bill, she supposed he was speaking of Patsy—whoever she was.

"You don't think he will be in the way?"

"No, why should he be? Perhaps you would like to go with me too?"

If she were honest with herself, she would like to go, if for no other reason than knowing confused thoughts would be marching through her mind the entire time he was away.

"Okay."

"Just okay, no questions, no arguments?"

"I can change my mind."

"No, I want you."

Those few simple words settled in their heads, causing them both to feel the need for a change of topic.

"We'll leave after breakfast. I'll take my Lincoln instead of the pickup."

Austen didn't even know he had any vehicle besides the pickup. Where did he keep it? Maybe he had a driver too. Seemed like the more she learned about him, the more there was to know.

Even after being introduced to Patsy Thomas—a young girl about ten years old with coal black hair and dark brown eyes, Austen was still unsure of Mark's relationship to her. When they met at the airport, there were only hugs, each telling the other, "How good it is to see you again." Could she be his daughter? If so, why hadn't he said? And wouldn't there have been a more affectionate greeting? She looked closely at both of them, trying to find a resemblance.

Maybe she would know by the end of the few days' visit, especially since they would be living in the same house. Patsy had a cellphone and talked to someone regularly. Austen couldn't help wondering who, where, and what did she talk to them about?

She and David became fast friends, and at the Friday Night Feed they were running around, meeting all the other kids who were enjoying the night with their families. They were even helping Kate and Bill as they brought out food and served it. When the band played, they held hands and danced around with laughter. Watching them, Austen made note of the distinct difference in their coloring—Patsy's dark hair and eyes, next to David's blonde hair and blue eyes—the same as his father's. Passing through her mind was the question of what coloring there would be in a child of hers and Mark's.

Austen had heard Patsy addressing Mark by his name, and when she asked her why, Patsy replied with, "David calls him Mark."

"But that's different; isn't Mark your dad?"

Giving her a puzzled look, Patsy said, "No; if he was, David and I could be brother and sister!"

Then they ran back into the crowd, looking for Kate and Bill.

She froze when she heard a hearty laugh behind her and turned around to see Mark with his annoying grin.

"Why didn't you just ask me?"

"I tried to, and I know you purposely led me on. You're good at that."

"Oh, I'm glad to be good at something," he returned as he began to close the space between them.

Turning, she made to move away.

She wondered often these days where this teasing man had come from. She remembered Bill telling her that first morning that Mark was usually so calm, he was dull. Mark was certainly not dull anymore—neither was he calm, at least not around her. But would she want him to be dull? Would she want him to be calm?

What would it matter anyway? She really had no hold on him, but admitted to herself that whatever, however he was, she did want him. Knowing she wouldn't be there to experience any of it, she began to cry.

By then he had reached her, and almost automatically gathered her into his arms. He had no idea why she was crying; was it his teasing? And why was he teasing? Maybe it was a defensive thing so he wouldn't be serious. Why did his heart hurt to see the tears, and where had that soft heart come from? And what was he going to do about it? Summer would soon be gone, and so would she.

She let him hold her for awhile, and tried to pull away when Patsy and David ran up wondering what had happened.

Mark assured them she was okay, just a bit tired. Then, keeping her in his arms, they joined all the others who were dancing. Austen thought, if this is to be all there is, then so be it.

"Can you tell me why you were crying?"

"No, I can't; being tired is as good a reason as any."

He twirled her around, then back into his arms—a couple of steps, a pause—then they stopped moving, each gazing into the other's eyes before abruptly separating.

Kate and Bill had been watching, surprised when Mark danced her into the crowd, and, giving each other a look, wondered if finally the two were accepting their mutual feelings. Then saw the abrupt end to the temporary respite in the clash between the two.

It was only later that Austen realized she still had no clue about the relationship between Mark and Patsy.

When the evening activities had ended and they had returned to the house, Patsy asked why they didn't sleep together. Her mom and dad did. What a question from a ten-year old. They didn't even try to explain; it would take too many words. Besides, both of the kids were wilting from all the exuberance of the evening, she probably wouldn't even remember by morning. But returning to Austen's mind were her earlier thoughts about a possible child.

Saturday was the first time Patsy had a chance to go on the trail, which had been the main reason she wanted to visit. Again, Austen was wagon master for a group, so Patsy and David were both with her. It didn't take long for her to realize that Patsy wasn't an amateur, maybe just a bit out of practice. As if she had once done all the jobs as a regular routine, creating more questions for Austen. She even knew about the fire pits, but didn't have all the strength needed for digging a fresh one.

At the end of the day, she offered to let Patsy help drive the wagon. Patsy accepted immediately, saying, "I haven't gotten to do this before." She was so excited, Austen had to calm her down so Jack and Jennie wouldn't run away with them on the wagon seat trying to hold on.

Supper that night was fashioned from food prepared by Kate and stored in their refrigerator. Thank goodness for Kate; Austen wasn't sure what they would have eaten most days if not for her. It seemed that in years past, Mark usually ate with the Pearsons after returning from a trail ride. So perhaps one might consider it usual for Kate to provide their meals. Even though they didn't often eat together, Mark still shared the same food.

On that Saturday night, they all gathered around the table, with Austen dishing up the macaroni and cheese, salad, and sourdough bread. Patsy had set the table ahead of time, and it was reminiscent of a family, with the four of them. All the while, Austen was still puzzled about the relationship between the two Thomases. What a diverse group.

She wondered if the quiet evening was courtesy of the fact that Patsy was there, though she had thrown in some awkward statements and questions since being with them. Whatever the reason, she welcomed it.

And it continued to be quiet, with only a little conversation between Mark and Patsy, who seemed to be learning what was happening in each other's lives. Whatever the relationship, they didn't seem to get together often.

Patsy had seen Austen with her crossword puzzle book, and said, "My grandma likes those too. Do you know her?"

"No, I'm afraid I don't."

A baffled look passed over her face, as if she was trying to figure out something. Then she said, "Isn't she David's grandma?"

It seemed, bright as she was, family relationships were still beyond her grasp. And of course, in this case there wasn't one.

Mark came to her rescue, saying, "David has a different grandma. Now it's getting late, and time for you young ones to get in bed. Tomorrow will be another full day, starting with church."

Austen had looked forward to each of the church services this summer, which gave an opportunity for a more serene, quiet ambiance, filling her with a peace that soaked into her being. If only she could absorb it so that it wouldn't be overrun by Mark's potent presence. There was such a powerful charisma about him; her nerves were always in an uproar.

As she waited for the service to start, she thought how different—and safer?—it would have been if Bill was the person in charge, as she had first believed. David would have been comfortable in his company, and she certainly would have. But reminding herself how her son adored Mark, she had to be honest, believing it was a good thing, even with the constant knowledge it was only temporary.

The band was warming up, and she found herself singing along with them. Josh was there for the service, and upon hearing her suggested to the band that they have her lead. She was reluctant, but did know most of the words of the hymns and praise songs, so finally agreed, not knowing if this was a departure from normal.

She was not completely unaccustomed to performing in front of a congregation. In the past she had been in the choir, and was part of a praise team for her home church. She had also been in various music groups in high school; plus, she and some friends had formed a trio that performed at churches and intermissions for school plays. She had missed being able to continue those activities the past few years, and welcomed this opportunity.

She hadn't rehearsed with the group, but was confident and said a silent prayer before services started. Song sheets had been passed out to the good-sized group. Many of them belonged to the congregation of the pastor who was doing the service.

Thankfully, Mark had been in the background during the exchange between her, Josh, and the band. But along with everyone else, he was soon made aware of her presence in front. She had taken time to let the kids know what was happening and asked them to be good and sit quietly, but to join in when they knew the songs.

It had always been easy for her to move between alto and soprano, but depending on the song, she loved to just harmonize. And the praise songs that day allowed all of that. She didn't overpower any of the other parts, and all their voices blended wonderfully. Since she was already familiar with the songs, her eyes were often closed, her face reflecting the joy she felt.

After finishing the four songs, she returned to her seat with Patsy and David. The two had been attentive and joined in when they knew the words. Then Mark appeared, and all of her calm serenity disappeared.

"Is there anything you can't do?"

"I don't cook much."

"That's okay, I do."

She tried to concentrate on the words of the sermon, which was difficult since because of the crowd. Mark was pressed up against her. Why hadn't he chosen a seat on the other side of the kids, or in the back where she couldn't see him?

Later, Patsy asked when they started holding church services. "I like it," she said, "but what happens if it rains?"

Austen had wondered the same thing but hadn't asked, thinking it was kind of nice to have an uninhibited child along who pretty much voiced whatever was on her mind.

"We started services about five years ago," Mark said.

"David must have been a baby."

"Yes, I guess he was," he said, glancing at Austen.

"If we know enough ahead of time that there's a possibility of rain, we put up a big tent. Only a couple of times have we had to cancel."

Members of the band came up and asked Austen to join them for the next service, which would be the last—the day before Labor Day. She glanced at Mark before answering, and he nodded. So, even knowing it would be just a couple of days before she would leave, she agreed.

Then they added, "Maybe you can join us for some of our gigs?" looking back and forth between her and Mark who said, "Well, I don't know about that. You know she's my employee; would you pay me a user's fee?"

He was smiling as he said it, then noticed Austen's face. She had paled with hurt and anger.

Fourteen

Mark could feel Austen withdraw, though there was no movement. Waving the band away, he took her hand, which she jerked out of his grasp then told David they were going back to the house, though she didn't really want to. Right now she didn't want to be near anything that reminded her of him.

Looking up, she saw Kate heading toward her with her arms out, and ran into them.

At the same time, Bill came up to Mark, who looked more than forlorn.

"What did you do, boy?"

"I made a stupid remark."

He had tilted his hat in such a way that his eyes couldn't really be seen, but Bill was sure he saw tears.

Through all this, Patsy and David stood silent, holding hands as they looked from one adult to the other.

Kate motioned for them to come to her, then they all headed toward the Pearsons' home.

Thankfully, none of the others in attendance, except the band, had any idea of the unusual occurrence.

Bill was trying to remember what activities were scheduled for the afternoon. For now, at least Mark was beyond taking charge. He looked worse than the day his wife left—or more accurately, didn't come home. He had seen Kate taking the other three to their house, so he suggested to Mark they go to his.

Austen was thinking the next few weeks couldn't pass quickly enough. Maybe she and David could move into a cabin, or maybe the Pearsons had an extra room.

At her house, Kate turned on the TV and found something both of the kids would watch, then sat Austen down at the table and began gathering the makings of a meal.

Austen asked if she had any extra room—or even a couch she could use for a month.

"I don't think that will be necessary. For now, let's make lunch."

"Do you know what he said?"

"I don't, but I did see his face—whatever it was, I think it's affected him as much as you. Fact is, I think he was crying."

That surprised Austen; she couldn't even imagine seeing him cry. That thought softened her feelings and she began to think she may have overreacted. He had been smiling when he said those hurtful words.

At Mark's, Bill poured a cup of cold coffee and warmed it up in the microwave, then brought it to him.

"Okay, what did you say?"

When Mark told him, Bill said, "No wonder she reacted like she did. Gonna take a while, maybe a miracle to get over that. She may even decide to pack everything up and take her and David back to Kansas."

Mark thought back to the day his wife didn't come home and how that had affected his life the last several years. But that feeling was nothing compared to what he was suffering now.

Patsy had texted her parents that Austen and Mark had a fight. They texted back, wanting to know, "Who is Austen?" to which Patsy replied, "David's mother."

Now more in confusion than not, Matthew tried to text Mark to no avail, then texted Bill. Bill answered but didn't elaborate, just told him to call Kate, who could give him some answers.

Kate answered Matthew's call and withdrew to another room so she could talk freely. "This will take a while; I'll keep it as brief as possible."

She told Matthew about the day Austen had arrived, then gave him a history of Austen and David. "Ever since that first day, there has been constant dissension between the two adults, but Mark and David have become great buddies. I think they adore each other; David is only four years old, by the way.

"Fact is, Bill and I would both tell you that although it's obvious to us they each have strong feelings for the other, they are doing their best to do nothing about it. Now today after our church service, Mark made a comment meant to be humorous, but she didn't interpret it that way. She and the two kids are here; Bill is at Mark's house with him."

In reply to Matthew, she said, "No, Patsy hasn't caused any problems. They've all been getting along well together.

I'm going to talk to Austen, same as I'm sure Bill is talking to Mark—we're trying to talk some sense into them.

"You should have seen him lately. He's back to the Mark he used to be; completely opposite to the way he was the day Austen came. And we love her, just about as much as we do Mark. We want to see them together—they need and deserve each other."

As she waited for Kate to return to the room, Austen contemplated what a bewildering day it had been—starting out so good, then being able to sing again—leading to that remark Mark had made. Maybe she had acted without thinking, but the words had struck her as cruel—more than teasing, at least in the way she saw it. It had been complicated enough being around him before; now in this new situation, she wasn't sure how things would be between them.

When Kate came back, she said to Austen, "I'm going to tell you something that Mark probably wouldn't want me to. I know you have heard certain comments and even seen expressions pass over his face at times that don't seem to have any interpretation."

"Before I tell you that, I think you've been wondering about the relationship between him and Patsy. She's his niece; his brother Matthew's daughter. They live in Lincoln. Used to come pretty often, but not the last few years."

"I remember watching your face when Mark said something about coming back. He was married; they were young, had known each other a long time—I believe like you and your husband? But she didn't like it here; despite the family history with TW, she hadn't expected to have to live here. Added to that, Mark wanted a family and she wouldn't consider that at all—didn't want to ruin her figure, mostly. But she would have been a terrible mother," Kate said, then taking hold of Austen's hands, added, "not like you at all.

"One day she went on a shopping trip to Scottsbluff; no one noticed that she had packed most of her clothes and took them with her. She didn't come back—Mark didn't hear anything from her for almost a month; then he got divorce papers in the mail. Hasn't seen her since. So that's the man who greeted you when you arrived." She saw that Austen was wiping tears from her eyes.

"He's changed so much since you and David have been here, back to the Mark we used to know. I know he hurt you badly—probably because you love him."

At that, Austen gave her a started look.

"But try to forgive him. He's worth it."

"Whew, glad to get that off my mind, I've wanted to tell you for weeks. Now I need to finish lunch and find out if the men are going to join us."

Mark was remembering when he first saw Austen, and all the times in between. They had developed a friendship; no, it was more than that, but he had refused to admit it. He hadn't wanted to ever have any serious relationship—once was too much.

He hadn't been able to stop his pushing and teasing. And remembering those few more intimate contacts at the beginning of summer made him ache thinking about them. If he didn't want—why did he feel?

"Hate to interrupt your thoughts, but is there anything scheduled for this afternoon?" Bill asked.

"I think there's a short trek, just a few people. One of the other hands should be able to take care of it. I'll call him."

"Okay, then, just had a text from Kate and she's fixing lunch, so let's go."

Mark went, not knowing Austen and the kids would be there. Somehow he hadn't even thought about where they might be.

He checked his phone and saw that his brother had texted him, then said to Bill, "Guess I better get back with him; he's probably wondering how Patsy is doing."

Bill told him, "Kate took care of it."

Mark gave him a 'look' but chose not to question him.

Just before they got to the house, Bill told him, "Oh—perhaps you need to think up a good apology."

Meanwhile, Austen was thinking that whatever the final result, she wasn't going to let him get over it easily. Maybe things would be a bit less distracting. Then again, she realized that her thoughts shouldn't matter anyway; they wouldn't be together much longer.

The kids had fallen asleep leaning against each other, so they had to be wakened for lunch. And because the adults were all immersed in the subdued atmosphere, Patsy and David provided most of the conversation at the table.

When all were finished eating, Kate and Bill took the kids to Plattsford for ice cream, leaving Mark and Austen to resolve their dispute.

The two were separated as far apart as they could be and still be in the same room. Both were filled with emotions that they were still trying to camouflage.

Finally Mark told her, "You were so good today with the band. I shouldn't have been surprised; and even if you say you don't cook, I doubt there's anything else you can't do. I've been amazed at how well you learned everything needed to be a good wagon master—actually, a great one. And those stories…"

He was slowly walking toward her as he talked. "I've teased you to keep from letting things get serious. You probably know I haven't wanted to get serious about anyone ever again."

She wanted to move, even as she waited for him to reach her. When he got to her, she let him take her hand.

The whole time he had been talking, she kept remembering what Kate had told her.

"I'm so sorry I hurt you. I don't ever want to hurt you."

He was trying to hold the tears back, but couldn't. Austen teared up as well.

"My feelings were probably too close to the edge. I forgive you. And though your teasing usually irritates me, I think I like it," she said.

But there was a change after this incident and they weren't sure what the next few weeks would bring, but certainly they'd be different than the past few. Despite hugs in previous times, there were none now, just smiles and a pat on the back.

Still, Austen at least, thought, that's not what I want. There's too much sadness in this; what can I do about it?

"Can we still be Mr. Thomas and Mrs. Wiley?"

He couldn't help smiling as he said, "Yes."

Because of the way the day had progressed, they had no vehicle, so walked to Mark's house. They had texted Kate and Bill to let them know they were home and could drop the kids off when they came back.

The atmosphere in the room was as if all life had been sucked out of it. Hopefully that would improve when the kids got home.

But there wasn't time for change; Patsy and David were beyond exhausted and needed to go to bed. But since David had hardly seen Mark that day, he ran to hug him around the legs, and said, "I love you, Mark."

Picking him up and giving a warm hug, Mark said, "I love you too, cowboy."

Fifteen

$\mathcal{A}$usten had forgotten to ask Bill about the availability of a cabin for the next week, so, first thing on Monday morning, she texted him to say she had two friends planning to come the next week for a couple of days, and hoped there would be a place for them.

Everything continued to be subdued in the house, with the adults eating on their own, but making sure the kids had something. Mark told Patsy it would be good for her to get her things together for leaving the next day, and to make sure she didn't forget anything.

Both of the kids were puzzled about what had happened and what was happening. He told them it was because they were going to miss Patsy, but that didn't address her worries.

As far as trail work, other hands would be taking care of the longer treks planned for the day. Mark, Austen, and the kids were scheduled for a two-hour trek in the afternoon. So that still left the morning to get through.

Occasionally, the two adults would steal glances at the other, each wanting to break the spell, the silence, and not being sure how to achieve that goal. Mark went out to check that all was well with the other drivers, almost wishing he was one of them, yet not really wanting to put a lot of distance between him and Austen, hoping they could get past the standoff.

A family with two children, an eight-year-old boy and a six-year-old girl, were their trekkers for the afternoon. Their joyous exuberance helped to allay the unfamiliar restraint of the wagon master and crew.

To add to the upheaval, Mark's parents, John and Mary Thomas, had decided to make a surprise visit. They hadn't been there for trail season in a while, and knowing the season was winding down, expected there wouldn't be many guests. Though they kept in touch regularly, Mark had not shared anything about Austen and David; nor had Bill and Kate, who also kept in touch with them. Thus, they expected to stay at Mark's house.

They flew into the airport at Scottsbluff, rented a car, and drove into TrailWays and Mark's house mid-afternoon. His house was never locked, so they walked in, heading toward the extra bedrooms. As they entered, they saw Austen's and David's things, which brought a puzzled look to their faces. What did it mean?

Dropping their luggage in the living room, they drove to the Pearsons', who were as surprised to see them as they were at seeing the evidence of someone occupying a section of Mark's house.

Kate asked, "Did Mark know you were coming?" And thought to herself, probably not, or he would have 'warned' them, wouldn't he?

Their query regarding the luggage and other items at Mark's was directed at Bill. Not quite knowing what to tell them, he simply said, "Well, he hired a family this year, and you know they usually stay at the house."

John asked, "Wonder if it will be too much trouble to move them to a cabin? How many are there?"

Both Kate and Bill were uncertain how to answer, being sure Mark wouldn't move the two, despite the confusion of the day before.

So they simply said, "You'll have to ask Mark."

By the time the trail group returned to headquarters, that distressing turmoil was lessening; though there had been no Mrs. Wiley-Mr. Thomas moments which somehow exemplified a normal day and Austen almost looked forward to those teasing instances.

The senior Thomases were watching when the wagon came to a stop, as did Mark, who was on his horse. Patsy jumped down, and the family exited out the back. Mark dismounted and reached to help David off the seat, but stopping Austen, who had started to get down on her own. Setting David down, he turned to her, offering his hand, saying, "Mrs. Wiley."

When she reached the ground, she stumbled against him—perhaps on purpose. His arms went around her and they briefly hugged. She nodded at him: "Mr. Thomas." Then finally there are smiles. Maybe a breakthrough?

He reached to take off her hat and pulled out the pins holding her hair, letting it tumble down her back, eliciting a gasp from Mark's parents, who continued to watch. At that, Bill and Kate grinned.

"I like it better down," Mark told Austen as he placed her hat back on her head and put the pins in his pocket.

David and Patsy saw the change in the adults and started dancing around them, David taking Mark's hand and Patsy grabbing Austen's.

He had not seen his parents, but they had watched the scene with Austen and the kids. They had not realized the driver was a woman, but when they did, noted he was paying extra attention to her, especially when he released her hair.

Those people must be the family that is staying in his house. Then they realized the little girl was their granddaughter. Well, they had intended on surprising Mark—and he surely had surprised them.

Turning to Bill and Kate, John said, "Looks like we might need a cabin after all. Is there one available for the rest of the week?"

Mark, Austen, and the kids walked on up to the Pearsons' since they expected to have a meal there as per usual. Seeing the car parked in front, Mark wondered who it might be. Maybe a guest who had come to spend the night before going on the trail tomorrow?

When they walked in, he came face to face with his parents. Patsy cried, "Gramma! Grampa! What are you doing here?" and ran to them for hugs.

That was enough to answer the question as to who they were, which was running through Austen's mind. Had Mark expected them?

Mark still had David's hand in his as he greeted them, "Mom, Dad. Why didn't you let me know you were coming?" So that second question was answered.

"We wanted to surprise you," his mother told him, "which I guess we have. We didn't expect to be surprised by you."

They continued looking from Mark to David to Austen, waiting for him to introduce them.

Finally, over his initial shock, Mark told David, "These are my parents, John and Mary Thomas," and to them, "This is my friend, David Wiley."

David gave them a shy grin, saying, "He calls me cowboy."

Then pulling Austen forward, keeping his hand on her shoulder, "And this is David's mother, Austen. They're staying at the house with me."

Kate and Bill had kept a close eye on the four throughout the introductions, not being able to gauge what Mark's parents were thinking.

Mostly what they were thinking was how beautiful Austen was, and how much Mark seemed to care for her and her son. They were happy to see the new personality, so different than when they had last seen him. If it was due to the Wileys, they were grateful.

Kate called them for supper and they all found places at the table, with Mark, Austen, and David together, and Patsy making a place between her grandparents.

Bill said grace, then Kate brought the bowls of food to the table. Mary asked Patsy how long she had been there and what she had been doing.

"I came Thursday and have to leave tomorrow. I got to go on the trail and even drive Jack and Jennie. We had a big feast on Friday, and church yesterday. Austen even got to sing with the band. And David and I danced Friday night. I think Mark and Austen did too."

"Sounds like you've had a great time," Mary said, to which Patsy nodded and smiled. She was too busy eating to say more.

Turning to Mark, his dad told him, "We had expected to stay at the house, so our luggage is there. I asked Bill if there might be a cabin available for the rest of the week." He glanced at Bill, who nodded.

"Good, we'll retrieve our stuff when we finish here and know where we'll be."

Mary said, "Wish we could have longer with Patsy."

"Maybe you can go with me when I take her to the airport tomorrow," Mark said. His parents quickly agreed.

Turning to Austen, Mary asked, "How do you like the work on the trail?"

"I love it. Never had the chance to be outdoors so much. Had to learn everything; think I've been the dumbest trail hand your son has ever had," she told her at the same time catching Mark's eye.

"No, actually, she's probably the smartest one I've ever had," Mark countered.

His parents could see there was a special connection between the two, while at the same time they sensed an underlying sadness. Maybe Kate and Bill could fill them in on whatever it all meant.

The next day, Patsy's grandparents had driven to the house and were helping get her luggage in the car. David wondered why she couldn't stay, and Austen told him that she was going home to her mommie and daddy.

Before leaving, Patsy wrapped her arms around Austen, giving her a warm hug, then said to her, "When you and

Mark get married, you will be my aunt and David will be my cousin. Can I be in the wedding?"

Seems she had figured out something about relationships; if only that would happen. Austen didn't know that all the adults, including Mark, had heard her statement, each pondering it in their own way.

Then Patsy hugged and kissed David, telling him, "I'm glad I got to know you. Didn't we have a lot of fun?" David only nodded, then grabbed his mother's hand and clung to it as if he was afraid she was leaving too.

Since his parents could provide transportation to the airport for Patsy, Mark wanted to stay to begin the overnight trek with Austen, who would be leading. This was more out of a protective feeling than anything else, since he had no doubt she was capable of taking care of everything herself.

"I think it will be good for you to go with them. It'll give you a little more time with Patsy; and on the way home, with no young ears listening, you can tell them all the trouble I've caused you", smiling up at him as she finished her statement.

"Okay, Mrs. Wiley, but rule or not, take your cellphone with you so I can keep in touch in case something happens. And be careful."

"I'll take one of those cowbells I saw in the tack room and ring it if I need help. Besides, if something happens, we won't be that far away from headquarters. And what help would you be in a car thirty miles away?"

"I wish you would take it anyway, in case I want to get in touch with you," he told her. "As soon as I return I'll come to the site. I'll remember to bring my bedroll and a tarp so I can sleep under the wagon."

"Very well, Mr. Thomas, I'll be waiting for you."

He seemed not to notice her teasing demeanor.

Just as she knew they would, his parents had lots of questions about her and David. He gave them a brief history of hiring Austen, making them laugh when he explained how he'd thought he was hiring a man.

They thought how wrong that was, and she was a beauty at that.

"And ever since I decided to let her stay—you know we had never made a practice of hiring women—we seem to be constantly at odds, though I think we like each other. David and I have been close from the start."

"She wanted to be able to spend more time with him, and I believe she resigned from a good job to come here. We've hardly talked enough for me to really know what kind of job it was. And I hadn't thought about it, but guess she will have to look for a new job when she gets home."

"So where is she from; and what about David's father?"

"She's a city girl from the Kansas City area. And David's father was killed in a car wreck when he was only six months old."

He had become almost reflective as he conveyed the information to his parents, realizing that after all this time he should know more about her.

His parents watched him as he talked about their relationship, which reinforced their belief that he more than liked Austen. Why did he think they only liked each other? It only took five minutes in their presence to know differently. What on earth was he going to do about it? It was like he didn't want to admit his feelings. Was his failed marriage the reason?

His mother blurted out, "Well, why don't you just marry her? Then she can stay here and won't have to look for another job. I think Patsy had the right idea. Don't you know that when you talk about her, your whole being is almost glowing?"

Mark was driving, and his mother's outburst startled him. Didn't she remember what had happened before? He couldn't go through that again, though remembering those occasions when Austen first arrived that could so easily have developed into something more, he almost ached. And the thought of her leaving affected him the same way. What was he to do? For now, he pretended he hadn't heard.

His dad, who was sitting beside him, had said nothing, but Mark noticed the twitching of his lips, indicating he was amused. No doubt he agreed with his wife.

When they got back to TrailWays, he quickly changed clothes, grabbed his bedroll and a tarp, and saddled his horse to head toward the site for the overnight.

As he neared it, he saw Austen and Josh in a close conversation and laughing. "Must be funny," was the first thing out of his mouth.

"Good to see you too, Mr. Thomas," she said, sounding hurt. Mark thought, I've done it again.

In truth, he had wanted to say something about Josh's flirting and thought better of it. Still feeling on the outside and no right anyway. How many weeks left—how could he stand it—what was he going to do about it—what did he want to do about it?

There would be only one more Sunday church service with her singing again, and that thought reached down into his soul. How could he bear it? Maybe Bill was right, and his mother—maybe she would stay. But he couldn't survive having her for a short time, and then lose her.

Austen's voice broke into his introspection, "I told him about my friends coming next week, and that one of them is a teacher. He was telling me about some of the pranks his students have pulled."

Josh had been watching both of them, and thought, these two have got to resolve their differences. Then he took off, telling them, "I'll see you tomorrow, in case there's some mail to go out." He got on his horse and headed back to headquarters.

Mark put his bedroll and tarp in the wagon Austen was using, then took a ride around to see how things were going. It was apparent everything was well organized; two tents had been pitched and the pit had been dug for cooking; some were even working on that activity. She had learned so well, she could probably teach new hands. Maybe he should find out what her job had been. Did it in some way mesh with what she had been doing this summer?

After the meal, the fire was banked so as not to create a fire—no other light except the moon which was not full; but still provided illumination. One of the hands, who was also a member of the band, had brought his guitar, and everyone gathered around for a song fest. Mark could not imagine why, but Austen chose not to join in, remaining in the background and heading toward the wagon to prepare for sleep. Could her decision have something to do with that disaster on Sunday?

As soon as he had seen Mark, David came running up, telling him, "I thought you left."

"Hey, cowboy, I would never leave without telling you goodbye."

"I don't want you to say goodbye."

Those words caused a lump in Mark's throat; how could he deal with that? It was going to happen soon. He asked the boy what he had done during the day, distracting both of them from the poignant thoughts.

With David beginning to droop, Mark told him, "Looks like it's bed time." Then, just as Austen had, they headed toward the same wagon.

David asked him, "Are you going to sleep with us?"

Without thinking, Mark said, "I'd like to." And David smiled, saying, "Goody!"

When they arrived, he saw that Austen had made sure his things were near the opening so he would have no need to enter. Looking toward the sky, he thought it looked like rain; it might be a wet night. But he spread his tarp anyway, checking for rocks and anything that might cause an uncomfortable bed. The bedroll went on top of that, planning to wrap it around him if he got cold. Seeing what he was doing, David asked about it.

"You and your Mommie will sleep in the wagon, and I'll sleep underneath."

Jumping up into it David asked Austen if he could sleep under the wagon with Mark. She knew he would be safe, but hadn't checked the sky.

"Yes, just stay with him and do what he says." She handed her son's bedroll to Mark, then settled where she had prepared her bed.

Mark couldn't help smiling as he told the boy, "First thing we need to do is put our boots and socks inside the wagon so no critter will crawl into them."

Under the wagon, David had barely got under his cover before falling asleep. But after his long day, Mark lay awake with troubling thoughts swirling around in his mind, especially after what his mother had said to him. Then just as he drifted off, it started sprinkling, and he was awake again.

He thought at first it would clear up, but it was soon pouring down. Even if it stopped soon, he and David were already soaked. He gathered their bedding, except for the tarp, and draped it onto the wagon seat, then, helping David, they climbed into the wagon. Austen had not been aware it was raining, so she woke up confused. Though she couldn't see it, she could almost feel Mark grinning.

"Hey, cowboy, you need to take off your shirt and pants; then maybe you can crawl in with your mommie."

"There's an extra quilt," Austen said.

"Only one? Maybe he can use that and I'll crawl in with you." Seemed like his teasing had returned.

David was down to his underwear and shivering, and his mother told him, "Come here, sweetie."

She was glad there was no light so Mark couldn't see her blushing face, as she knew he too would be taking off his shirt and pants the same as her son.

"You probably can't see anything, but you might want to keep your eyes closed anyway because I need to strip too."

She didn't need light—her imagination was enough to visualize his skin under his shirt, and knew it wouldn't be easy to push his tight jeans—even tighter, being wet—down and off his legs.

He spread the wet clothing on a tool rack in the back of the wagon, hoping it might dry at least a little before morning. He felt around for the extra quilt, wrapping himself in it, then fumbled about trying to find a place to settle without being too close to the other two. The rain falling on the roof of the wagon provided a soft background, and the three drifted off to sleep.

During the night in their tossing and turning, still wrapped in their quilts, Austen ended up against Mark, both of them relaxing into a deep slumber. One of her arms was around him, the other pressed against his back. Then, still asleep in his quilt, Mark turned, wrapping his arms around her. Despite his intentions the night before, somehow he had located his quilt next to hers. With the quilts between them and completely covering them, there was no other contact, but it was an intimate situation they hadn't expected.

It was probably a good thing that David happened to wake up first, excited that they were all together in the wagon. He and his mother climbed out of their quilt and she checked his shirt and pants. They were still damp, but not so much that he couldn't get into them. Checking Mark's clothes, she looked his way only to see that his eyes were on hers.

"Are they dry enough?"

"The shirt probably is, but I don't know about the pants." She could almost picture him struggling to get into them.

"Maybe you should call Bill and ask if he can bring me a dry pair."

Going through her mind was what would everyone think about his need for a pair of pants, especially his parents.

He could sense the wheels turning and said, "Why don't you toss them over here, then turn your head. I'll see if I can struggle into them."

It took a while, but he was able to do so, then told her, "You can look now," which she did. "Kind of tight, but maybe they'll stretch out after awhile."

His pants were on, though not yet fastened, and he was still shirtless. How many times had she imagined what that bare skin would look like, would feel like?

"Want to touch, Mrs. Wiley?"

Yes, she thought, which she was sure he knew. She didn't have to say it out loud. And looking at his unshaven face, she remembered how she had felt that long ago morning when she had first seen him. Strangely, even though they lived in the same house, she hadn't seen him since those first few days when he hadn't shaved. He made sure that was taken care of before leaving his room. Was it because he knew how it made her feel?

Now she turned away, telling David, "Let's get your boots on; we need to start the morning." And she was gone from the wagon before Mark disturbed her even more.

After breakfast, Mark rolled up all the bedding and the tarp, and because his wet pants were uncomfortable, started back to Headquarters telling Austen he would return before they broke camp.

Sixteen

The next day was Thursday, and a free day, making a good opportunity for a visit with Mark's parents. John wanted to look over all the property, buildings and fields, animals, and equipment. He and Mary hadn't been there for some time, but he had been in charge for years before retiring and was curious as to whether there had been changes.

Mary thought the day would present a chance to become better acquainted with Austen; by now thinking/hoping she would be her daughter-in-law some day.

They drove to Mark's house, wondering whether they should knock, but he was opening the door just as they reached it.

"Mom, Dad, are you ready for the tour? Thought we would ride."

His mother said to him, "Well actually, if it won't bother Austen, I'd like to stay here."

Austen and David were still at the table where they had just finished breakfast. When he learned the men would be riding around the property, he wanted to go too. Mark looked toward Austen with a silent question.

"He can go if you think he won't be in the way."

"He's never in the way. Get your boots on, cowboy, you can ride with me."

David still had trouble getting his boots on by himself, so brought them to Mark to help him. While doing so, Mark told him, "You know, we need to see if there's a David-size saddle around here somewhere and get you on a horse by yourself. But that will have to be another day; no time for lessons this morning."

John and Mary had paid special attention throughout the exchange between the two, noticing how gentle and patient he was with the boy, just as a good father would be. They both began to think their son definitely needed a push, something to open his eyes, maybe his heart, remembering how it had been broken a few years before. But they would only be there a couple more days and weren't sure if they could influence him. Wondering also, why was their smart son being so dense.

As the men were getting ready to leave, Austen gave her son a kiss; then Mark came close and asked, "How about me?"

It was like he had forgotten his parents were just inches away.

Unable to help herself, she asked, "What would you do if I did, Mr. Thomas?"

"We'll have to check it out sometime, Mrs. Wiley."

David was looking back and forth from one to the other, as were Mark's parents.

Breaking eye contact, Mark told David to get his hat, and when he came back the three headed out the door. Bill had saddled three horses and had them ready. Since Mary wasn't going with them, Mark and John asked Bill to join them.

Unexpectedly, Austen was feeling desolate after the challenge with Mark, and their standard Mr. Thomas and Mrs. Wiley. The teasing usually lifted her spirits, filling her with a certain contentment. Did this new sentiment that overcame her mean her heart was accepting the fact her time at TrailWays would soon be at an end and their relationship would never be more than what it was now?

She had turned away so Mark's mother wouldn't see the tears welling up in her eyes, needing time to gather her composure before facing her; not realizing that Mary was well aware of it all and would have liked to wrap the younger woman in her arms.

What had happened to that stubborn woman who had arrived at the end of May? That woman could be aggressive—and was. Maybe it was time for her to become more assertive; but that didn't really fit her personality. She couldn't see Mark responding to someone chasing him, having seen him ignore several women who had flirted with him through the summer. And despite her anguish about the current situation, she didn't want to be ignored.

"Why don't you greet him with a kiss when they return?"

Austen was taken aback at hearing Mary say that, and, turning, told her, "We've never kissed." But she had memorized his face and remembered those other times when they had been so close to kissing, thumbs rubbing across her lips, and the longing she had felt.

"Oh my, won't it be a surprise," Mary said, echoing Austen's own thoughts.

It should have been uncomfortable sharing this with Mark's mother, but her words of affirmation brought a more contented mood to Austen. And as they cleaned up the breakfast things, she continued to contemplate Mark's return.

His mother mentioned that the dishwasher had been added since they left, but mostly the kitchen was the same.

As they began the tour of the house, Austen told her, "I like the house; it's warm and comfortable, though I've only been in Mark's wing briefly. Once David took a nap on the couch in his office, and one day, without my noticing, he took off to find Mark, who had left the house. When I realized he was gone, Mark's office was the first place I looked."

"Seems like your son likes my son a lot," Mary said with a smile.

"Yes, he adores him. Since his dad died when he was a baby, he hasn't actually been around any man except my dad. And Mark has been patient and loving with him from the first time they met." Pausing briefly, she added, "I don't even want to consider how he will react when we leave and he won't have Mark anymore."

Mary could almost feel the grief, love, and concern in Austen as she shared her uncertainties.

"The desk in there could be a twin to one I have at home."

As she said those words a wistful look crossed her face that was not lost on Mary. Was it because she was homesick, or because she wanted to stay?

"I want to check in there later; maybe you will join me?"

"Now, if you don't mind, can we look in your rooms? Just curious about any changes that might have been made."

"Of course; my things and David's are in there, if only temporarily. I have to tell you, it's not real neat right now," Austen told her as they walked in. "I'm working on a project that's taking up some space."

The first thing Mary noticed was a sewing machine, some fabric spread out, and what looked like the beginnings of a dress.

"I haven't mentioned it to Mark. I got the fabric and pattern when we went to Scottsbluff with Kate, then borrowed her sewing machine. I'm working on making a dress to wear for Sunday church, even though there's only one left for this season." "I'll probably just leave it when I go back to Kansas. I was thinking it could be the beginning of a wardrobe made available for people to wear on the trail."

"I don't know about my son, but I think it's a great idea. There are people who like to dress in period clothes for activities they're participating in." Mary continued, "I never did much sewing, but my mother was a wonderful seamstress and made many of my clothes when I was growing up. Think I'm actually envious of those who can do that."

"My mother is also very talented. I learned to sew, and when I was younger I even made some of my own clothes. Sometimes I liked it and sometimes not, but I should be able to finish this dress without a lot of problems."

Before she completed her perusal of the room, Mary noticed a crossword puzzle magazine. Picking it up, she asked Austen, "You're an enthusiast?"

"Yes. Have been since I was very little and noticed an uncle working a puzzle in a newspaper. Actually, I think they're good for building one's vocabulary."

Smiling, Mary told her, "It's one of my favorite pastimes, and I agree about the vocabulary."

When they finished in their wing of the house, Mary headed for Mark's, and persuaded Austen to go with her.

The first thing Mary did was head for the desk which had been mentioned earlier. It had been her desk for a brief time before they retired, and then it became Mark's. She wanted to see if the items she had left in the drawers were still there. Finding what she had specifically hoped to, she brought out a scrapbook, then called Austen over. It contained school reports, pictures, and newspaper articles, all relating to Mark. He had been a cute little boy with dark hair, much like Patsy's, making Austen wonder when the silver hair had appeared and if something occurred to change it. Both John and Mary had only silver streaks going through theirs. Mary put the scrapbook back and checked a few other things as she glanced around the office. Stepping into his bedroom and looking around, she commented, "It's pretty neat; guess I taught him well."

Austen thought briefly about the one time she had been in the room when Mark was showing her around. Now there was a pair of jeans on his bed—maybe the ones he had worn two nights before when he had ended up in the wagon with her and David.

"Tell me about your desk."

She was glad for the interruption. "My husband, Don, and I found it at an outdoor flea market not long after we were married. It required lots of work and time to get it in good shape. We had planned to furnish an eventual home with antiques. That was the only piece we had."

Mary noted there was a certain sadness, but mostly from a cherished memory.

When they finished with the inspection of the rooms, they checked the refrigerator and freezer to see what was available for lunch, deciding that grilled cheese sandwiches and soup would suffice; but waited for the men to return before beginning preparations.

While the ladies shared thoughts, memories, and wishes, John and Bill were plying Mark with encouragement to concentrate on the woman who was living in his house and what he planned to do regarding her and David. They hoped to convince him it wasn't fair to them to continue in his present actions. If he couldn't admit his true feelings and ask her to stay, then he should stop the teasing innuendos.

He brought up his failed marriage, to which they both told him she was nothing like Tricia. Don't let something that happened five years ago keep you from the happiness you deserve and add more despondency to Austen.

They returned to the house; Mark was glad for the outing to be over. He resented the other men having taken the occasion to point out what they considered his unfeeling treatment of Austen. How else was he to behave toward her? No matter how he really felt, he couldn't let himself act in response to the strong attraction that washed over him every time he was near her. It had taken too long to get over the breakup of his marriage, and he didn't want to chance that again.

As he entered the house, both Austen and his mother made note of the irritation on his face; wondering what could have caused that look. Probably didn't bode well.

David ran to his mommie to give her a hug. Then despite the daunting look on his face and before she lost her nerve, Austen walked to Mark, put her hands on his shoulders, and, on tiptoe, gave him a peck on his lips. "There's your kiss, Mr. Thomas."

She meant for it to be only that and started to pull away, but after his initial surprise, Mark gathered her into his arms, pulling her as close as he could, and with his lips over hers, said, "That was no kiss, Mrs. Wiley."

Beginning tentatively, he initiated a kiss unlike any she had ever known like one she had only dreamed about. Her arms reached around him as the kiss deepened and she tried to get closer to him.

The room and all that was in it faded away; all their frustrations and longings of the past several weeks rose up in them. And even as the kiss ended, they still stood with arms wrapped around each other, leaning into each other, no words, as both were taken by surprise at what it had become. He hadn't intended for that to happen, and, truth was, neither had she.

Did they react that way because they were heart hungry? Neither had been in a relationship for a time, though their awareness had been building since that first day. It was as if they were hungry for each other. She was sure she had heard that whispered, "pesky mosquito," and remembered the previous times those words had passed his lips. Was there some meaning to them?

John and Mary had taken David outside to give them privacy. Mark's mother almost ached watching them, recognizing that some of their yearning that had built up the last few weeks had spilled out. But what might be the ultimate outcome? Could they finally resolve their fears and accept their love for each other?

When they reentered the house, Mark and Austen were still close, but no longer touching, seeming not to know what to do next. Their strong reaction to the kiss was unexpected.

How might it affect the next few weeks? Austen thought she needed to decide if she could accept what had been the status quo of their relationship. Or should she decide this was the best it would be, and slowly retreat from any relationship? Not that there had been one.

Mark had not expected the deep feelings, especially after the advice his dad and Bill had plied him with when they were out. Maybe they were right. If anything, he wanted to draw closer to her, but to what end? He knew he wanted to repeat that kiss. She would be leaving in a few weeks; would he be able to bear it when she was gone?

Truth be told, would either of them be able to suppress the strong feelings expressed in that kiss?

When David came in with Mark's parents, he ran to his mother and Mark, wrapping his arms around their legs—a timely interruption leading to their separation.

Austen remembered that she and Mary had planned a lunch, and, almost in a daze, started toward the kitchen. Mary then told her, "Kate called, said she is bringing fried chicken, potato salad, and even chocolate cake for lunch. She and Bill will join us."

During the meal, David and the older adults provided all the conversation; the little boy was still excited about all he had seen on the tour around the property. Austen and

Mark continued to be quiet and subdued, occasionally taking a fleeting look at each other across the table, as if they were still experiencing those strong feelings that had arisen with their kiss. The older adults wondering if they tasted anything of their lunch.

With his meal finished, David was ready for a nap and wanted to sleep on Mark's couch. Mark told him, "Come on, I'll get you settled."

Kate and Bill gathered up the bowls from lunch and headed home while Mark's parents said they, too, needed to rest and were going back to their cabin saying they didn't know whether they would see them before the next day, leaving them alone together to contemplate the future.

With no cleanup to distract them from what had occurred earlier, Mark and Austen moved to the couch and actually sat together. He reached for her hand, which she let him take. It was too early to go back to the attempt to ignore what had previously been normal.

Mark asked her, "Do you want to talk about it?"

She shrugged, wondering how that kiss could be labeled "it."

"You know, those 'old people' left us alone on purpose." He continued, amused by her questioning look, "Made me feel like a little kid needing some instruction."

"You called them old people, though I think that's a bit insulting. None of them seem old to me. How old are you?" It was something she had wondered ever since that first day; this seemed to be an ideal time to ask.

"What's that got to do with anything?" Mark asked.

"I would just like to know."

"How old are you?"

"I asked first."

She tried to remove her hand from his hold, but he only held it more firmly.

"I'm thirty-two; so now, how old are you? Think I asked you that question once before, wondering if you're old enough for me."

"I'm twenty-eight; is that old enough?'"

"It's perfect."

Throughout the banter, Mark would occasionally raise her hand to his mouth, kissing her fingers.

"Want to talk about it yet?"

"What would that accomplish? Let's just accept that we kissed; and not only that, your mom and dad and David all saw it. That fact can't be changed."

Mark told her, "I don't want to change it."

She made no reply, though she felt the same. She wanted another one—no, not just one. She wanted it for everyday—occurring naturally, just as if that was the way life was supposed to be.

Then, bravely, she brought up a sensitive subject: "I know about your marriage. I can't change what happened with it, any more than I can change the fact about the death of my husband. They were both sad events in our lives; and until I met you, I had no plans to change anything. But we still have life and feelings and deserve to love. And I want to love—didn't think I ever would again."

She could feel him withdrawing, though he still held her hand.

"If that scares you, I'm sorry—I can't help how I feel. And I don't know why I brought it up now—I just felt compelled."

Though she expected it, he made no response except to squeeze her hand. She didn't know what that meant.

Still sitting silently, he released her hand, placed both of his on her shoulders, and turned her toward him. With a sad smile on his face, he hugged her, but still no words.

Then he asked, "Want to go to church with me Sunday? You've met some of the people."

That was not what she expected. Was that where he went when there were no trail events and no services at TrailWays? And why the invitation now?

"That would be nice; what time, and what should I wear?"

"We need to leave here by eight thirty, and you can wear basically the same thing you wear on the trail."

"Now I'm going to take a nap, too," and headed for his part of the house.

She lay down for a while, but wasn't able to sleep, so she worked on the dress she was making. With plenty of time to wonder about what was going to happen to the relationship—whatever kind it was—with Mark, she wondered if he would move from his teasing to something more serious. She realized she hoped not; the teasing was better than nothing; at least he was expressing attention.

Seventeen

There were a couple of short treks on Friday. Austen was in charge of one, and another hand led the second. Mark had taken the day off to spend more time with his parents, who would be leaving the next morning; and because he didn't have any trail duties, he also kept David.

When her trek was completed, someone else took care of Jack and Jennie and cleared out the wagon so she could have a respite before the evening activities. One of the band members had asked her if she could join them again. She texted Mark for permission and he agreed, even adding, "Besides, I love your voice."

There was time for a shower, and she left her hair down, although she would wear her hat when she joined the others. Mark's demeanor was the same as it had been since 'the kiss', but everyone else noticed that just as before, he couldn't take his eyes off of her.

As usual for Friday night, cars, pickups, even horses were arriving, filling the parking lot, discharging people who headed for the dining area. Austen and Mary joined Kate in helping serve. Some of the people who came every Friday night greeted her as if they were old friends, asking how the summer was going for her and what she would do after Labor Day. She shrugged, since she didn't really know.

As the number of people in line became fewer, Mary looked around for her husband, who had been keeping an eye on David. He had claimed a place where they all could sit, even Mark if he needed to. David had climbed into Mary's lap when she sat down. She hugged him, thinking he already seems like a grandchild to me. None of them knew where Mark was, but he usually milled around, making sure all was going as it was supposed to.

His parents, as well as Kate and Bill, checked over the crowd and saw both Mark's ex-wife, Tricia, and Lissa Courtney, who seemed to be looking for someone—probably Mark. In an effort to protect Austen and Mark, they planned to keep an eye on the two women and somehow ward them off if they approached either of them. Why was Tricia here? She hadn't been around since she drove off and didn't come back. And hadn't Mark told Lissa to stay away?

Because he was keeping such a close eye on Austen himself, Mark hadn't seen either of the women. And the task the others had taken on themselves became a bit more difficult when she moved through the crowd to join the band.

 She had become a favorite with many of them and they greeted her as she headed to the stage.

On a whim, Tricia had thought to attend the Friday Night Feed. Mark's family had initiated the event just before she left. Since then her life hadn't quite been what she had expected it to be, nor had she seen any of the Thomas family.

But TrailWays seemed to have become quite successful. She had learned that Mark was still single—which to her meant he was still in love with her. Even though she had not liked being there, she could probably learn to bear it. She expected that Mark would still be as handsome as always, and was anxious to see him.

Just as Austen reached the band, Tricia reached the Thomases. Mark wasn't there but since his parents were, she anticipated he would soon join them. She said a snide hello, as if she saw them every day. When Mark saw her, he was somewhat taken aback. David was still on Mary's lap, and Tricia said, "What a cute little boy. Who does he belong to?"

"Me."

David flashed his sweet smile at Mark and wrapped his arms around his neck. Mark gave him a hug, said, "Let's go see Mommie" then set him down, all the while ignoring Tricia.

Mary asked her, "Why are you here, Tricia? I thought you had sworn you would never set foot here again."

"Well, you know how it is; people do change their minds now and then."

But who really was the little boy Mark had walked off with?

She had dressed very carefully for her expected meeting with him: fancy western duds, hat and boots, and her hair arranged in a complicated 'do'. Looking at her, Mary thought she certainly couldn't compete with Austen.

Still standing where Mark had left her, Tricia turned to see where he was headed, and wasn't completely surprised as he reached the stage. He used to have some notion of playing with the band; maybe he still did. She decided to head that way herself and see what transpired.

Mary had expected Tricia to leave as soon as she heard Mark claim David as his own, but it troubled her that she was headed toward the stage too. She hoped Bill or Kate would notice and try to obstruct her progress.

Checking for Lissa's location, Mary saw that she too was moving toward the stage area. Somehow without being aware, Mark had passed by her. Austen was there and told the band if there happened to be words in a song that she didn't know she would "la la" through them, drawing a laugh.

When she got out of her car, Lissa had immediately looked around for Mark. It had been a few weeks since he had indicated she shouldn't return. But Friday nights were for everybody and she had been wondering what was taking place there. Maybe that little widow had grown tired of the work and left by now. Also, in her mind, he would have become tired of having that little boy hanging on to him too. She was sure that someday, Mark would become tired of living alone. They had known each other and done business together for years. It would be natural for them to be together, even if he didn't know it.

John had been keeping a close eye on Lissa, so he situated himself to waylay her as she moved toward the stage.

"Hello, Lissa."

"Mr. Thomas, how are you? Haven't seen you for awhile."

Without answering, he questioned her, asking, "Weren't you asked not to return?"

Austen noticed her—and another woman she didn't recognize—both openly trying to catch Mark's eye. She also saw that he was paying them no attention, as if not even aware of them. And both of the women, separately, had recognized some individuals from one of the Scottsbluff television stations and wondered why they were there. Each was also thinking it would be fabulous to have a reunion with Mark, and have it be broadcast so their friends would see it.

She hadn't seen him all day, but there he was, holding David's hand as they neared. Their eyes caught and a smile spread across his face—a real, sweet smile, not a teasing one that she had seen so often. It was as if he were telling her how special she was and how glad he was to see her.

She returned Mark's smile, then looked past him and saw his father with Lissa. What did that mean? She told herself not to think about it. Mark was there, coming closer. As he and David got to the stage, David wanted to go to his mother, and the band members told him, "Come on up. You too, Mark, if you want to."

To Austen's surprise, he did. After seeing Tricia he wanted to be close to her, as if needing to protect her.

David ran immediately to his mother, wanting a hug. It was then that the other women took a close look at her, Lissa finally recognizing that it was the little widow, while Tricia was still baffled.

Mark told her, "He missed you today," looking as if he wanted to kiss her as he had the day before.

One of the band members asked for attention from the rest of them, including Mark and Austen. "Before we start, we need to tell you that one of our recent visitors is a reporter for a TV station in Scottsbluff. He asked about doing a story on TrailWays, and I told him yes."Turning to Mark, he said, "Hope that's okay. I would have told you sooner, but had no idea they would be here tonight."

"Do they expect to be filming tonight?"

"Don't know, guess we'll have to wait and see."

"Should be okay; we sure don't want to create a negative situation."

"Great. Okay, people, It's almost time to start."

The band members had noticed the exchange between Mark and Austen, so they asked, "Want to join us? David, you can too."

At that, Austen gave them all a puzzled look. She watched as Mark walked to a guitar on a stand at back of the stage, picked it up, and strummed through the chords to be sure it was tuned before joining the band. Her look changed to one of surprise and amazement. He flashed that annoying, amused grin she had fallen in love with so many weeks ago. He walked to her, tilted his hat over his eyes, then asked, "Wanna sing with me, Mrs. Wiley?"

The usual Friday night activities were taking place when the band leader made introductions.

"Some of you know her; for those who don't—the beautiful Austen, her son David, and, of course you all know Mark!"

During the applause and whistling, Bill picked David up and took him to where he and Kate and Mark's parents were sitting.

Austen had expected she would join them for a couple of songs, but people were slowly deserting the other activities to find a seat near the band. She and Mark stayed on the stage, joining in all the selections, from old time western songs to gospel to top-ten country hits. One of the songs was "What If I Never Get Over You," which made her think of her relationship with Mark. She knew she would never get over him and prayed that somehow there wouldn't be a time she would need to try to.

Their set stretched into the evening, and intermissions were necessary. At those times, Mark would make his way to her, seemingly needing her touch. Even during the playing and singing, he regularly sent his sweet, loving smiles her way.

It had been exhilarating being on stage with Mark and the band, but also exhausting. Of course she couldn't have had any such inkling of this opportunity when she'd applied for the job.

When Mark was introduced, she had seen Lissa and that other woman trying to get his attention. During one of the intermissions, she saw they were gone. Mark's parents, as well as Bill and Kate, had watched them go and hoped that was the end of that, whatever that was.

She told him about seeing them "looking at you like you were some prize they wanted to chase down. Do you know who the other one was?"

He didn't want to tell her that it was Tricia, but maybe she needed to know. He would tell her later. Now he only said, "You're the only one I want chasing me." He had been shocked to see Tricia, but realized there were no feelings other than he was glad she wasn't around anymore.

"And what about you playing the guitar? Why haven't you mentioned it before?"

"A man has to have some secrets."

Even as he said it, he thought maybe it was a mistake not to tell her who Tricia was.

Eighteen

ark's parents had an eleven o'clock flight the next day and planned to leave TW at nine. Bill and Kate had invited them, as well as Mark, Austen, and David to have breakfast with them.

There was much discussion around the table about the previous night. It had been a wonderful evening, even with the appearance of those two women. Mark and Austen received compliments on their appearance with the band. Because their extended presentation had turned out to be such a popular addition, his dad said, "Maybe you should add music nights separate from Friday nights, perhaps monthly. You and Austen could be the stars."

At that, Mark and Austen gave each other a long, searching glance. Despite their recent amity, there still was no indication that their time together would last beyond summer. His parents were disappointed to note that those two had reverted to their previous behavior toward each other. Apparently that kiss yesterday had not led to another; maybe there would be no more kisses at all.

The conversation turned to the appearance of the television crew. To Mark's dismay, Tricia was included in the discussion. She had been seen hanging around the crew, per-haps even being interviewed. There was fear she may have voiced misinformation which would be detrimental to Trail-Ways and to Mark. Especially since she had been diverted from the family earlier in the evening.

John asked, "But what can we do about it? They probably want to air it soon."

Bill said, "Only thing I can think of is to have Larry get in touch with the person who contacted him and ask what we might be able to do. I'm sure they wouldn't want any neg-ative response from us; and if something was recorded that might turn out that way, they may edit it."

John and Mark nodded, and Bill told them, "I'll contact Larry now. Probably not a good idea to sit on it."

Larry Brown, the unofficial leader of the band, agreed to check on the subject immediately and let them know what he found out.

Austen listened to the discussion, wondering if Tricia was the other woman she had seen; if so, what was her con-nection to TrailWays and Mark? Though she was beginning to have a good idea, the main thing that bothered her was that Mark hadn't told her, and probably wouldn't. She turned to him with a troubled look on her face.

If they were to make their flight, John and Mary could wait no longer to leave, though they were reluctant to do so in the middle of this quandary. Hugs and kisses were shared all around. Mary told Austen, "I am so glad I got to know you. I hope there will be many more times for us to be together."

By now there were almost tears in Austen's eyes. She wondered what would be the outcome regarding Tricia, and she was still afraid to look forward to a future with Mark. So all she said was, "Me too."

To David, they said, "Take care of your mommie."

Smiling, he said, "Okay."

They were all standing near the car when John asked Bill to let him know what happened; then after another round of hugs, they were on their way.

There was a poignant silence when they left. Strangely, Austen thought to herself, "I'm going to miss them more than I do my parents." Probably because she had come to love them, and harbored a dream of being part of their family—a dream she didn't have much confidence in.

The three were getting ready to drive back to Mark's house when a call came from Larry. He told them that if someone would drive to the TV station that very afternoon to meet the producer, they would be able to preview the footage planned for a broadcast the next day.

Mark grabbed Austen's hand, then asked Kate and Bill if they could take care of David the rest of the day. He wanted to make the trip and take Austen with him. Besides being able to check the tape, he wanted to straighten some things out with her and thought it would be easier if it were just the two of them.

The Pearsons readily agreed and began thinking about what they could do to entertain him. David said, "Maybe we can make cookies."

Bill gave Mark the name of the contact at the station as well as his phone number so he could let him know he was coming. They both hugged and kissed David, told him they loved him and to be good for Kate and Bill. Then after more hugs, they were headed down the drive Mark's parents had taken a short time ago toward Scottsbluff.

It was a quiet ride, with Mark working out in his mind how much to tell Austen about Tricia. She barely knew the basics. He had married young, just as she did, but he hadn't been wise, hadn't looked beneath the surface to see the real Tricia. He hadn't listened to his parents or heeded their advice.

Starting with that information, he continued, "She knew I planned to stay at TrailWays and maybe eventually be in charge. She knew I wanted a family. But, just as my parents warned me, she wanted no part of TW, and no way did she want to be saddled with a family."

"I still wouldn't look past her beauty," he said, stealing a glance at Austen, and knowing Tricia didn't even have that.

"I was young and stupid, sure she would change her mind, and I was egotistical, believing I would be enough to hold her. Then that day came when she drove away and didn't come home. That woman last night was Tricia, and it was the first time I had seen her since."

Sensing that he was emptying his heart and soul reliving those days, Austen kept quiet and prayed as they moved down the highway. If he hadn't been driving she would have reached for his hand.

"I have no clue why she was there. Mom was holding David in her lap when Tricia came up; didn't have much to say, but did ask who he belonged to. I told her 'me,' then took him to the stage so we could be with you."

"If she was interviewed, I wouldn't be surprised at anything she would have said."

He didn't add that because of those bad decisions in the past he was unable to make heart decisions now, and avoided situations where he would need to. Until Austen.

Now all she said was, "Thank you," figuring nothing else needed to be said. Except she did add, "No more secrets?"

"Maybe. Don't you expect some mystery?"

"I was astonished at the guitar playing!"

By then they had arrived at the TV station, and he told her with his teasing smile, "You'll just have to wait to learn about that."

The producer was waiting for them, and introduced himself as Jackson White. Mark shook his hand, telling him, "I'm Mark Thomas, owner of TrailWays, and this is my assistant, Austen Wiley."

When had she become an assistant? Maybe another mystery to be cleared up.

Jackson invited them into a room where the taped material was ready to be shown. It was well into the film when Tricia's face appeared.

Interviewer: "Have you been here before?"

Tricia: "Believe it or not, this is my first time, but I'm expecting to be here every week from now on. Mark Thomas and I were once married," she said, flashing a fake smile. "We were so young, and it didn't work out. But neither of us is married now, so we're renewing our acquaintance. Watch for an announcement." She smiled again.

A "congratulations" came from the film crew.

Austen had almost gasped as Mark groaned and reached for her hand.

Then, unexpectedly, a few minutes more into the tape, and there was Lissa. "Oh, I've known the Thomas family for years and have attended many Friday Night Feeds. Mark and I have been friends, and as an antique dealer, I have found many of the items he has used on his trail experiences. Now it's growing into more than just friendship." She smiled snidely.

The producer had not reviewed the tape, and after Lissa's appearance, shook his head in disbelief. "Okay, is any of that true?" He had been at the event, but not involved in the interviews.

As an answer, Mark took hold of Austen's hand and asked, "What do you think?"

Taking a closer look at her, the producer exclaimed, "You're beautiful Austen!"

Giving her a look that most people would have called loving, Mark said, "Yes, she is."

Surprising herself, Austen was blushing. She wasn't accustomed to receiving such open admiration.

Jackson told them, "I have an idea, if you two agree. How about we tape an interview with you now? Then we and the viewers can learn firsthand about TrailWays, and maybe your relationship?"

Still holding hands and with a silent question between them, Mark said, "An interview about TW fine, but no relationship questions."

Seeing their evident affection for each other, he wondered why, but agreed to TrailWays questions only.

Mark told him, "Not that I don't trust you, but I want to see for myself that those other interviews are destroyed."

The producer smiled and nodded as he began the interview, knowing that even though there would be no overt questions, the camera could pick up a lot.

He began by asking Mark, "Tell me a little about TrailWays."

"My folks began the trail events when my brother and I were in high school—moving away from ranching—about sixteen years ago. They learned early on it was best to keep the events between Memorial Day and Labor Day."

"I believe you're in charge now; when did that start?

"About five years ago. My folks were ready to retire and I was here. We had always thought my brother, Matt, would be the one to take over, but he wasn't interested. He's in Lincoln now."

"Any regrets?"

"No, I love it. It's part of me."

"I think it was at the suggestion of Bill and Kate Pearson that we started the Friday Night Feeds."

"And who are the Pearsons? Are they still with you?"

"They more or less serve as managers. They worked for my folks, and yes, they're very much with me. They'll be at TrailWays as long as they want to be. They're more like family than employees."

The producer told them, "After experiencing the Friday Night Feed myself, I'm wondering when it started? From what I could see, it's a popular event. Did it begin that way?"

"No, it didn't have very many customers at the beginning. There have been more people this year than ever."

"To what do you attribute that?"

"Maybe Austen's participation."

Jackson turned to her. "So how long have you been with TrailWays?"

"Actually, just this summer."

"Had you visited here before?"

"No." She looked questioningly toward Mark, as if for permission. He nodded his head, so she continued, "Fact is, I answered an ad for a hand—someone who liked history."

Mark added, "There was a lot for her to learn, and she did. She's probably the most determined person I've ever known."

Jackson continued, "So if you haven't been here long, how did you happen to become Mr. Thomas's assistant?"

She was glad Mark answered. "Because she's been invaluable in so many ways, and has imperceptibly initiated some new things into the business on the treks, as well as the Friday night events."

The interviewer asked, "What about the band? It sure got a lot of attention."

"It was just spur of the moment, and could also be because of Austen's appearance. Someone even suggested we have a band night occasionally. We might think of that for next summer."

At the end of the interview, Jackson told them, "I would like to go back to those interviews with the other ladies. Is it possible they would have heard before the event of the planned appearance of the station?"

Mark answered, "No idea. As I told you, I hadn't seen my ex-wife since she left until that night. And the other woman had been told weeks ago not to come around anymore."

But the 'Feeds' are open to everyone. We don't have anyone checking who comes in. I know Lissa lives in Scottsbluff;

maybe Tricia does too. Could they possibly have heard it from someone here?"

"Hard to say. But the reporters were roaming, looking for anyone willing to share their thoughts. They could have seen that and made sure they were noticed."

As promised, he had not asked anything about their personal life, but had noted they held hands throughout the interview. He thanked them for coming in, telling them he believed the interview would add a lot of substance to the program. Originally they had planned to air it the next day, but it would instead air within the next week. He told Mark, "Be prepared to get calls."

They were hungry when they left the station, but neither wanted to find a place to eat in Scottsbluff, instead choosing to drive home, pick up David, and prepare their own meal—not a usual practice for them.

On their way, Mark said, "Dad and Bill are likely wondering what happened today. Why don't you text them to let them know."

"I have Bill's number, but not your parents'."

"Okay, I don't ever remember it. Guess we can call when we get home."

Every time he used the word home as if she really was a part of it caused a yearning within her. Would it ever be?

"You can tell me about the guitar playing later. For now, why did you introduce me as your assistant?"

"Aren't you?"

"How could I be? I don't know what your plans are for a day, never mind a week or a month, or a summer. You don't share that information with me, or how many people are expected for any of the activities. I don't know what you do or where you go when you're not at the house. I didn't know what was going to happen on July Fourth, and I don't know if there are special plans for Labor Day. Besides, as far as I know, you don't even expect me to be here after that day. If I'm not here, I can't be an assistant."

He had almost forgotten that assertive, stubborn, challenging woman he met at the beginning of the summer, but she was still here, sitting beside him in a car driving toward the house they had shared for weeks, or was it months by now? And he really didn't know why he said she was his assistant. Maybe because he wanted her to be, but was afraid to mention it since he couldn't bring himself to tell her how he felt even after that kiss they had shared—when was it, just a few days ago? And how else would he have introduced her—a hand he had hired for the summer who turned out to be so important to him he wanted her to be around forever.

Taking a quick look at her, and hearing the anguish in her voice, he knew he had to find some way to console her if that was possible. Talk about being stupid. Seemed as if he had learned nothing.

"If I wasn't driving, I would wrap you in my arms and give you another of those kisses like the one we shared. I don't ever want to hurt you, but it seems to come easily for me. You're more important to me than being a hand like any of the others. I didn't want to introduce you as that. Strange as it sounds, I guess I do think of you as an assistant, because we do share things. Maybe not always having to do with the business, but more important."

When he referred to the kiss, a longing rushed over her. Why could just the mention of a kiss trigger that kind of emotion? She yearned for another. But of course, it would be safe to refer to it when they were in a moving car.

"I'm sorry; though I know saying those words isn't enough and won't change the hurt. Please forgive me—again."

"I'll try, but it gets harder every time. Do you still want us to go to church with you tomorrow?"

"Why wouldn't I?"

"Because we seem to be good at falling into disputes. Church will probably be good to remind us we can forgive and be forgiven.

"Do you remember that my friends are coming next week? Then just one more week after that."

Watching him out of the corner of her eye, she was sure he clenched his mouth, as if to stave off any words that might come out. Did that mean that despite today and everything that had happened in the last few weeks, it all still meant nothing in the end? Was that kiss the only one she would ever receive? And was that the main reason he hadn't wanted to discuss any relationship in the TV interview?

Now she turned her head to stare out the window at the passing scenery, willing herself to keep quiet. One step forward, two back. He still seemed to be unable to open up to love—or to admit it. And she wasn't sure how much more her heart could take. Except for the fact that it would go against her principles to leave a job early, she would be tempted to leave the same time her friends did. They could caravan.

She realized the car had slowed down, and Mark was pulling onto the shoulder, which looked wider at that particular place. Mark braked and turned off the engine, then checked to be sure the road was clear. He got out of the car, walked around the back to her door, and asked her to open it. Then he unbuckled her seat belt, pulled her out, wrapped his arms around her, and started a kiss that made her forget all her recent fears and doubts. She returned the kiss which lasted until they heard the honks of a passing car.

Saying, "Remember that, Mrs. Wiley," Mark helped her back into the car, buckled her seat belt, gave her one more kiss, then went around to get in the driver's seat.

Before starting the car, he turned toward her, flashing one of those sweet smiles she had seen recently, then turned the ignition, carefully pulled back onto the highway, and they were on their way again. What was she to think about that? Was it going to make any difference in what happened the next few weeks? Did it matter? Maybe after all she was going to have to be content with the few kisses, smiles, and sweet words she had received and would receive in the next couple of weeks. But she wasn't ready to say "so be it" yet.

"So now, maybe I'm ready to hear about the guitar."

With a sideways glance toward her, he said, "When we were still in elementary school, Matt and I took lessons. He lost interest, but I had dreams of being in a band—maybe even one of my own. Can't you see me as a Rock Star?"

She didn't have to look at him to think that yes, and you would have been surrounded by bunches of screaming women, from teenagers to grandmothers.

"Matt being the oldest, we all expected that he would take over running TrailWays. But I kept practicing and got together with other guys—Larry was one of them, and Jim

Johnson, who occasionally plays with the 'Friday Night' band, and maybe for the Sunday services. We never had any real gigs, but liked to pretend we did.

"You may have guessed that I still join them sometimes—just for fun. Last night was the first time I've played with them for real.

"So that's the story about the guitar," he said, then asked, "What don't I know about you? I don't even know what kind of job you had."

"For now, why don't we keep that a mystery? There needs to be something you don't know about me."

"But I want to know everything about you."

Nineteen

David had enjoyed his time with the Pearsons, and Austen thought it was as if he had yet another set of grandparents. She knew he would miss them when they returned to Kansas. Unless they came to visit, she didn't expect to see them again. Despite what he said, she continued to have the feeling that Mark wasn't going to alter his thoughts concerning a permanent relationship. And she would settle for nothing less. There had been too many instances these past several weeks that could so easily have moved on to serious conclusions. But each time in her mind, everything reverted to what happened at their first encounter those many weeks ago.

Then she remembered that 'almost' kiss.

And thought, why am I even deliberating over this? One shouldn't consider a possible permanent relationship based on a couple of dreamy, tender kisses, no matter that they reached deep down into her being. And no matter what wise advice she gave herself, she craved time with him.

David had taken a nap while at the Pearsons', and was full of energy when they got home. So after they ate, Mark asked him, "Hey, cowboy, want to see if we can find a saddle your size?" his eyes purposely avoiding Austen.

And there it was again, that hunk of a man with her little boy doing things that a father would do.

If possible, she was even more confused than ever. If he didn't expect her to stay—why take time for the saddle now? Though she knew it would be a good thing for David, even if there would only be a few days to enjoy riding on his own.

After they left, she spent some time working on the dress, which was almost finished, then called her mother and texted both Jerilyn and Maggie.

Her mother told her, "You must know that you haven't included much in your texts. Like how you and Mark are getting along. Are he and David still as close as ever? What about his parents; are they as nice as he is?"

"Oh, Mama."

As soon as her mother heard that, she knew something heart wrenching would come out.

"We're still getting along about the same as when you were here, but I care more for him every day; and every day I tell myself not to dream about something that probably won't happen. We're still mostly calling each other Mr. Thomas and Mrs. Wiley."

"Right now he's out with David, looking for a 'David-size' saddle as he calls it. Apparently he expects to locate one somewhere at Headquarters. Maybe one he used when he was little. Then he plans to teach David to ride on his own. I don't know why he would bother with that if we're not going to be here."

"As for his parents, they were surprised that Mark hired a woman, but I have no question they cared for me the same as you and Dad cared for Mark. They actually treated David as if he were their grandson. And just as you pushed me, they pushed him to open himself up for love."

"He's told me more about his marriage, and I wonder if that's still affecting his reluctance to become serious about anyone else. His ex-wife actually showed up at Friday Night Feed last night. He hadn't seen her since she left. Have I told you that story?"

After relating it, she said, "Enough of that. A crew from one of the TV stations in Scottsbluff was here too. They did a lot of filming and a few interviews. It's probably going to be aired sometime in the coming week."

"You probably know that Jerilyn and Maggie are coming next week. Not sure what they might be expecting; but it will be good to see them."

She avoided telling her mother about the invitation to church, and wasn't sure why. Something about it seemed like it should lead to something more; but what?

~

They were back in the pickup for the ride to church on Sunday, where the Greeter told her, "Heard about the Lady Wagon Master. So glad to meet you and David. Are you going to be around for Labor Day?"

Instead of answering, she turned to Mark, who said, "I expect she will."

There were others inside whom she had met at Trail-Ways, including the pastor. "I remember you from the service. I'm Jerry Miller, and this is my wife, Shirley. So glad Mark brought you today."

She recognized the band members who were setting up, and seeing her, they waved. Those with families later introduced her to their spouses and children.

Another person who had entered the church but not yet found a seat said, "It's beautiful Austen," bringing a flush to her face, especially since several others turned her way.

She wanted to reach for Mark's hand to feel anchored, but he was visiting with others. She saw that David had reverted to the shyness that was so much a part of him when they first arrived at TrailWays. Before she could react to it, Mark had also noticed and bent down to ask if he wanted to stay with them, or go see some other kids. He chose to stay with them, which was fine with Austen, who was thinking he would be between them during the service.

She wondered if Mark went every Sunday when there were not services at TW. Those mornings were usually quiet and slow, since no activities were planned until afternoon. She had always tried to stay out of his space when both were at the house, so she didn't know whether he was there or not. And if he wasn't, she assumed he was more than likely taking care of whatever was needed for the business.

Mark broke into her thoughts when he introduced the sheriff. "Meet John Law. He and his deputies keep an eye on the place when we're gone."

The number of people entering the church had dwindled, and Mark, finally taking her hand, said, "Let's get a seat," leading her and David to a place near the middle of the congregation but on the end of the row. Then instead of having David between them, he seated him on one side of Austen while he chose the other side, and whispered to her, "in case he falls asleep, he can rest his head in your lap." He squeezed her hand, giving her that sweet smile that appeared so often recently.

Whether he realized it or not, everyone in the church was speculating that there would be a wedding soon; and didn't they make such a handsome/beautiful couple?

Just as the service at TrailWays that first Sunday had been a blessing for her, so was this one. She absorbed the words of the sermon, the prayers and songs, often with her eyes closed, as she let them reach inside her, giving peace. Her own silent prayer was that she could receive an answer to the anguish she felt about her relationship with Mark.

When they left, it seemed that every member of the congregation had told her they hoped she would come again. As they climbed into the pickup, Mark said, "It's a bit early for lunch, but how about driving around anyway and see if there's a place we'd like to eat?"

David had actually slept briefly, so he was full of energy. He asked about getting pizza. The adults smiled, and Austen expected that was what they would end up with. Instead, Mark took them to a restaurant where they could order breakfast or lunch, with lots of selections. The menu even included pizza, and though David checked out some of the other items, that's what he chose.

"What did you think of the service?"

"I enjoyed it. It filled my spirit with love and peace and comfort." She kept her eyes on him as she enumerated all the positive aspects that had touched her.

When the waitress brought their food, she said, "Hi Mark, is this your family?"

It seemed to Austen that everyone in the town must know him; but then, many people worked for him, and Trail-Ways had been in business for several years. He probably also had gone to school with some of them.

Mark's answer was simply, "Yes, Austen and David," he said, pointing to each of them.

Austen thought the waitress must not know him very well if she accepted that she and her son were his family. But none of this was helping her make any decisions. How could it when he alluded to their being his family and her his assistant, while at the same time not making any plans for them staying in Nebraska permanently, and almost pushing them away. He must be as confused as she; if only he would not be afraid to open up his heart.

Maybe she should take charge and just tell him, "We're going to stay here until you realize you want us here and can't bear to have us go. Hopefully it won't take much longer for you to get that fact through your head and heart."

Ha—as if that would happen.

When they returned to the pickup, Mark said, "Some people are coming this afternoon who want to shoot the cap-and-ball rifle. Do you want to come with me?"

No one had expressed an interest in shooting all summer, so she did want to watch and maybe try it herself.

"Yes, I do. I had hoped to be able to do that while I was still here," she said, glancing at him to see his reaction; there was none, as if he had willed himself to show no emotion. "Can David come with us?"

"Should be no problem. He's always so good about not being where he shouldn't be. Then maybe we can go horseback riding before dark."

"Do you mean me too?" He hadn't offered that to her all summer, and she found she wanted to.

"Can you ride?"

"I don't know. You've helped David; can't you help me?" She was actually glad when she saw his look of consternation. Maybe it would be good to take charge.

Those who came to shoot were two couples who had experienced the trail the year before. They hadn't met Austen then and weren't sure about her role. Instead of letting Mark introduce her, she told them, "I'm Austen Wiley and have been one of the wagon masters this summer; this is my son, David. And I haven't had a chance to shoot, so I'll be learning with you."

Looking at Mark, she saw that enigmatic smile was there, but with his hat, as usual, tipped over his eyes, she was unable to interpret his thoughts.

There were only two weeks left in the season for which she had been hired, so she decided she was going to voice her thoughts and feelings. When had she stopped doing that, anyway? Maybe even before that first breathtaking kiss.

The couples enjoyed the experience of shooting the rifles as she did too. Then when they left, Mark saddled up the horses. He had found the small one, so David would be riding by himself, though Mark wanted to stay near him in case he was needed. When Austen got settled, after some brief instructions, she took to riding as if it were part of her background. Two new things she had learned, and she thought, "see there, Mr. Thomas."

Kate invited them for Sunday dinner, and they were glad to accept the invitation. Austen kept thinking that since she worked so many hours, she had almost stopped cooking and wasn't sure she remembered how to plan meals. That wasn't really a good thing for either her or David. That would have to change when they got back to Overland Park, unless she got another job requiring those long hours. She realized her thoughts were returning more and more to the probability that she wouldn't be here. She had prepared some basic things, not much more than sandwiches, since being in Mark's house. She wasn't sure if he cooked for himself—perhaps in the "off season".

The Pearsons sensed the melancholy affecting Mark and Austen and wondered what it meant. They believed it had started the day before, with any contentment they felt slowly diminishing as if they were withdrawing from each other.

Twenty

The television station contacted Mark to let him know they would broadcast the episode on Friday night, meaning they and the Pearsons would need to record it. If others learned about the date of the upcoming airing, they might stay home to watch instead of attending Friday Night Feed, affecting the size of the crowd, which often was smaller that time of year anyway because summer was dwindling.

For the present, thoughts about that and any reaction to Mark calling Austen his assistant could be set aside as a new week began.

She completed the dress and returned the sewing machine to Kate. While there, she asked about what happened during the off-season. Did they take vacations, were there special projects or activities that occupied their time?

Kate told her that she and Bill were able to take off for a couple of weeks every year, which most often meant driving trips to National Parks and such. They also visited family; they had no children, but both had siblings, nieces and nephews, and cousins they didn't see often, though some of them had visited TrailWays in previous years.

"That's nice."

While Kate was giving her account, she noticed Austen wasn't paying much attention and rightly guessed she actually wanted to know what the owner of TW did.

"Mark pretty much stays around here, making sure everything is in good working order for the next season. Occasionally he considers possible new activities and how they might be initiated. He usually goes at least once to visit Matthew and his family in Lincoln, staying a couple of days. A few years ago, he went on a mission trip with the church."

"What about Christmas? Are there any activities here? Do you decorate?"

"Nothing special—most would no doubt describe it as dull or blah. Bill and I do have a tree; Mark doesn't."

She could see the sadness that moved across Austen's face and a perceptible drop of her shoulders, as if she could feel the bareness and emptiness in Mark's life. Kate realized that even she and Bill had missed that. What were they going to do about that boy? He still wasn't making a move to keep Austen and David with him. And they had brought him so much joy—almost as if he were a new creature. She didn't want to see him revert to the man he was before they came.

Austen changed the subject and the mood by asking, "Did you know I have two friends coming this week? Well, of course you do; you're in charge of the cabins."

Smiling, she went on, "I want to introduce them—well one, specifically—to Josh. I know they live hundreds of miles apart, but one never knows what might happen."

David had been watching television and came in carrying a picture he had seen on a shelf, asking, "Who is this?"

Kate looked at the picture of a young boy with dark hair sitting on a horse. "It's Mark when he was just a bit older than you are now."

The boy had a smile on his face. Looking at it, Austen saw the face of the Mark she knew with those sweet smiles she saw occasionally, and, unable to prevent it, there were tears.

Just then, Mark walked in and asked, "What's going on in here?"

Austen told him, "We're just discussing my friends' visit this week."

He had come closer, lifted her chin, and said, "Then why are you crying?"

"I'm not."

His look said he knew differently, but he didn't pursue it because David showed him the picture. "Kate said it's you."

"It must be if she says so. Looks like the saddle we found for you.

Not much going on today; want to go riding?" he asked, looking at both of them.

David was ready, but Austen told him, "I did enjoy it yesterday, and would love to another time. For today, I may just stay here with Kate. Not a lot more time to spend with her," trying to judge his reaction when she said it.

As had become usual these past few days, he acknowledged her statement with a blank face.

~

Maggie and Jerilyn drove in at five o'clock the next day, tired as Austen knew they would be. But there had been two drivers, and no young child necessitating more stops, so their trip had taken less time than hers had.

Austen had received a text from them, so she knew exactly when they would arrive and was waiting at the Pearsons' when they drove in. She introduced them to Kate and Bill, telling her friends that they were sort of substitute parents and she had leaned on them a lot.

Josh rode in just then, bringing letters from the trail to be mailed. She wondered if Kate or Bill had arranged that on purpose, considering what she had told Kate the day before.

Bill told him, "This is Maggie West and Jerilyn Tate, friends of Austen. I understand Jerilyn's a teacher, just like you."

"Ladies, Josh Wilson, our Pony Express Rider and general go-to person when we need help."

"Do you ladies have families?"

Maggie said, "I do. I'm married and have a boy who's six and a girl who's two."

"Not me," Jerilyn said. "Live all by myself, but I do get to take care of Maggie's and Austen's kids occasionally."

Kate added, "Josh is single too."

When had those two become matchmakers? Austen glanced at Josh and Jerilyn, who were smiling at each other as if it didn't bother them at all.

It had become normal for David to be with Mark, and they came in together not long after Josh did.

Bill took the responsibility of introducing Mark, then added, "Guess you know David."

His mother asked him, "David, do you remember Maggie and Jerilyn?"

He shyly nodded, still holding Mark's hand.

Kate told them all, "I need to show the ladies their cabin, and then why don't you all come back for supper—you too, Josh?"

Mrs. Morgan had said nothing to them about how handsome Mark was; maybe because she had so much to say about the tension between him and her daughter. So when Kate left them to get settled, they commented on seeing them together, but so far, no obvious tension.

Jerilyn said, "He's so good looking, it almost makes me hurt. And to think she's living in his house."

Then Maggie asked her, "What do you think of Josh?" To which she answered, "He's pretty cute too. Think I need to be around him more to make any deeper comment." Saying it in such a way that Maggie knew she had liked him instantly.

And after seeing David with Mark, they could see why that professor had believed they were dad and son; they were so natural together.

Conversation was lively at supper, with even Mark joining in. Periodically he would take hold of Austen's hand, turn to her, and smile. Her friends, as well as Josh, couldn't help noticing. He had watched the two all summer and wondered if Mark would ever come to his senses. Why was he letting something that happened so many years ago affect a loving life with her?

Josh and Jerilyn were seated across from each other, making it convenient to talk about their jobs. They shared details of some of the projects they had accomplished in the classroom, as well as antics of some of their students. She and Maggie shared more about the town where they lived than

Austen ever had; it was an informative, entertaining night for all.

Austen had asked them earlier about the possibility of going on the trail the next day. She would serve as wagon master, and Josh added that he would be riding for the Pony Express.

They enjoyed the short trek the next day, and when Josh rode in, Jerilyn had written a note to be mailed back home. He asked her if she would like to ride back with him, and to no one's surprise, she agreed. He helped her climb up behind him; then with her arms wrapped around him, they rode off.

Mark had ridden up about the same time to make sure all was well, he said, but his eyes stayed on Austen, looking as if he wanted to memorize everything about her.

Maggie told him that Jerilyn had made notes about several things she could use for instruction in the classroom, then added, "And there is so much I'm anxious to share with my family. Maybe we'll plan to visit for a longer trek sometime."

As soon as David heard Mark's voice he ran up to him, and when Josh took off with Jerilyn, Mark asked if he wanted to ride back with him. Austen helped him up, their hands brushing as Mark reached back to be sure David was settled.

Then saying, "Mrs. Wiley," and tipping his hat, took off in the direction Josh and Jerilyn had gone.

Maggie wondered about the "Mrs. Wiley," but said nothing. She vaguely remembered Austen's mother saying something about it when they had breakfast with her.

Austen said to her, "Looks like we're on our own. Anything else you want to do before we head in?"

"No, but I must tell you I have enjoyed everything; I didn't really expect to," she said with a smile. "And I would never have imagined you becoming such a professional with all that's required in this kind of job. Do you realize it seems natural to you? Was one of your ancestors a trail master?"

"It took lots of instruction and practice; Mark was quite a taskmaster. But it's important to do everything correctly and well," Austen told her. "Guess I'm surprised how much I enjoy everything about it. And before you ask, yes, I would stay if he asked; but if he doesn't, I won't come back another year."

"Are there any special plans for tomorrow?" Maggie asked.

"Not really; I've been thinking, but nothing has come to mind yet. We could take a ride into Plattsford to visit some of the businesses. Several of the store owners and managers are in the band. Maybe you and Jerilyn would like to meet them?"

~

When she told Mark she and her friends were going to drive into Plattsford, he asked if he could go too. Why, she wondered, but said she would ask them if they minded.

Of course they didn't mind, They wanted to spend more time seeing her and Mark together so they might gauge their relationship. What they had observed so far was slightly confusing—to them, anyway.

They were surprised the next morning when Mark and Austen drove up in a Lincoln to make the trip to the nearby town. David was staying with the Pearsons again, so it was adults only. When they got on the main road, Mark told them that Josh was going to meet them at the grocery store. The owner and his family also operated the caterers' wagon which provided food at the special events for TrailWays. Plus, the owner played guitar in the band.

They all went inside where the owner met them. "Hi, I'm Barry Cooper," he said, then drawing a woman to his side, added, "This is my wife, Linda. We've worked with TrailWays for longer than Mark has been in charge. Then, of course, there's the band. Mark practices with us a lot, but doesn't usually play at the events, or our other gigs."

Turning to Austen, he asked, "Have you told your friends about what happened last Friday night? This young lady is quite a vocalist, and when she and Mark joined us last week, people abandoned the other activities to listen to us as if we were giving a concert."

"Besides that, we learned that a TV crew was there, so we all felt like movie stars."

As he was talking, Maggie and Jerilyn first looked at each other with raised eyebrows, then back and forth between Austen and Mark. They were beginning to wonder if they really knew her. The stories they could tell when they were back home.

As she listened, Jerilyn was also looking around for Josh, wondering if he was really going to meet them there. Maggie and Austen were watching her face when she saw him come in; they saw the same expectant look on his, and smiled at each other as if to say it might be a successful match-up.

Mark had been watching as he listened to the dialogue between the friends, especially Austen's animated, happy, joyful, beautiful face. How could he bear to let her go? How could he not? He still couldn't accept that there might be a happy ending despite what so many others were telling him. They hadn't gone through the heartbreak he had. But, if he were honest, this would be greater.

Looking at Josh and Jerilyn together, he was jealous of their growing relationship—and in such a short time. He knew Josh had no broken relationships and guessed neither did Jerilyn. So their hearts were free to connect.

When they left the store, Josh asked if Jerilyn could ride with him so it wouldn't be so crowded. They had agreed to meet at the restaurant whose menu included breakfast all day, as well as many other options.

"Sure, man, we'll see you there."

Josh drove by his house and the school where he taught before heading to the restaurant, wanting Jerilyn to learn more about who he was.

Maggie was beginning to feel like the odd man out with the two couples. Josh and Jerilyn had just met, but were enjoying getting better acquainted and were thinking it might become a permanent relationship in a very short time.

She and Jerilyn also recognized the tension between Mark and Austen. And though they had pretty much lived together all summer, they still tiptoed around each other, both hurting, seemingly refusing to admit to the other how they felt. They could only imagine their heartsickness.

Josh asked the women how long they had known each other, and Maggie told him they had first met at church four years before, shortly after Austen's husband had died. There were several others in their small group who were all about the same age.

"Are the rest teachers? What about you, Maggie?" She said, "I'm lucky enough not having to work right now, but I was a church secretary. Three others are teachers, but you probably know what Austen did before she came here."

Mark said no, actually he didn't. He had realized weeks before that he had no idea what kind of job it was that she had quit to come to TrailWays. But he hadn't asked, by then believing it didn't make any difference to anything.

"Austen, do you want to tell them? I might not get all the details right."

"No, you know enough; go ahead."

"She had this great position with a big advertising company with lots of responsibility, but it wasn't an eight-hour-a-day job. Sometimes she even had to work weekends overseeing job completions. So she wasn't able to spend as much time with David as she wanted, and that, she felt, was important. You probably couldn't find anything more completely different from her responsibilities there. But she sure looks like she knows what she's doing, and I know she's happy being able to have David with her."

Mark was mostly listening, not contributing anything to the conversations. It actually surprised him to hear about what she had done—something fitting a sophisticated woman in the city, not someone who would dig pits for cooking and oversee a night on the trail.

"Do you all live in the same town?"

Jerilyn told him, "Well, if you can call Overland Park a town, we all live there, but not in the same neighborhoods. Church is our common ground."

He still had a questioning look, so she told him, "The city covers more than seventy-five square miles, and the population is almost two hundred thousand."

"I guess that is a little bigger than a town," Josh said with a smile, sending a contemplative look toward her as if wondering how someone from the city would fit in here.

When they got back to the cabin, the friends wanted to spend a little more time together, which gave Maggie and Jerilyn a chance to ask Austen how she really felt about Mark.

"No question, I love him; and frankly, I'm sure he loves me too and shows it in so many ways. Then he will pull back again. He has let his life be ruled by fear of rejection again, at least the part that has anything to do with his heart. If you had been here at the beginning of summer, you would recognize the major change that's occurred in him. Only thing that hasn't changed, he and David took to each other from the first moment they met.

"As things are, even now, I expect I will be going back to Kansas the day after Labor Day. And it's going to be so hard. I'm sure I can never love anyone else. And this love is so much different than what I felt for Don; maybe because I'm older and have experienced more life.

"The hardest thing is going to be telling David. He thinks Mark is his.

"So can we not talk about this again, and just enjoy the rest of our time together?"

Mark had delivered Maggie and Austen to the cabin and told her to call him when she was ready to come home; then he picked up David at the Pearsons'.

She called after another hour of reminiscing. When he got there, he and David went in briefly, and he asked the girls to come by his house the next morning.

"I'll make breakfast and you all can have a bit more time together before you have to get on the road."

When they got to the cabin, Mark told her, "I like your friends, and that matchmaking idea with Josh seems to have worked. Not sure I've ever seen him with that much interest in anyone, even when he's known them for awhile." He asked, "Do you miss your friends?"

"Of course I do; but we still keep in touch," she said, and, speaking before thinking, added, "Besides, maybe Jerilyn will end up here too."

He avoided responding to that statement. Instead, he asked, "Why haven't you ever told me about your job?"

"Why didn't you ever ask?"

"I'm asking now. From what Maggie said, it was pretty important."

"I guess it was; I had worked hard, had lots of special training, and my salary had increased significantly. But the hours spent were increasing too. There were times I wasn't able to pick up David until after eight o'clock. Sometimes I was even away from home on weekends.

"And before you ask, I don't miss it. It has been so wonderful having David with me most of the time, although, as you know, I obviously had no outdoors experience. But I've loved that part of the summer too."

He wanted to ask what she planned to do afterward, but didn't really want to know.

Mark had not cooked for her during the time she had been at his house, but he had told her once that he did cook—probably more in the off-season. The next morning, he made flapjacks, bacon, and eggs, and served coffee and orange juice—a breakfast evoking memories of her first morning at TrailWays.

When her friends drove off, she was unable to suppress her tears. But they were more for her and David and their impending departure than for her friends.

Twenty One

As had been expected, there were fewer people at the Friday Night Feed, partly because of the broadcast of last Friday night's activities. Some in the crowd indicated they were also recording it to view later. Other than that, it was pretty much as usual, the band playing without Austen and Mark's participation, and a more subdued atmosphere

She spent most of the evening helping Kate while keeping an eye on David and Mark, who invited everyone to his home the next day to watch the broadcast together. Since Barry was coming anyway, he was asked to bring a meal, including dessert, for all of them.

The band was especially pleased with the overall coverage, appreciating the way it was portrayed, which indicated how great they actually were. They thought it might lead to invitations to play for other events, and told Austen they needed her and Mark to join them. When the contribution of the Pearsons regarding Friday Night Feeds was mentioned, they all applauded. Kate and Bill stood to bow, pleased smiles on their faces.

Kate had to suppress a gasp when the interview with Mark and Austen flashed onto the screen. Their eyes kept returning to each other, the camera sometimes focusing on their hands, clasped together.

Mark left the room, unable to see this picture of his love for Austen; the others quieted their animated response to what they had seen since the beginning of the program.

Austen left, too, to start gathering plates and utensils for the meal, avoiding watching herself and Mark. It hurt too much. She kept remembering his stopping the car on the way home to give her that heart-stopping kiss. Such a short time ago; how she longed for more.

As the producer had expected, no questions were needed to be asked about a relationship. Kate thought there could be a still shot from the broadcast labeled LOVE.

"Mr. Thomas, you introduced Mrs. Wiley as your assistant. How long has that been the case?"

Eyebrows were raised when the producer made the statement about Austen being Mark's assistant, but Kate and Bill accepted it as fact, surprising Austen. If anyone knew what might be in Mark's mind and heart, they certainly did.

They had known for weeks—probably since the beginning of the summer—about the couple's feelings, but to see them on film confirmed it. They weren't all aware of the change that had occurred in the past week, but had sensed their withdrawal from each other, and wondered.

After seeing the broadcast, an old friend who once came regularly to the Friday night events called Mark, congratulating him on the success, then said, "I was surprised you have a female assistant. How did that happen? I remember in the past you wouldn't consider hiring any woman. Not that I think anything is wrong with it. And I must say, she's a beauty. What did they call her—oh, yes, Beautiful Austen. Anyway, don't think I can come this summer with just a couple of weeks left, but look for me next year."

Mark had introduced her to the producer as his assistant, not expecting it would become part of the broadcast. Now there were calls coming in, complimenting him on the activities, the band, and nearly always commenting on his lady assistant.

Mark was thinking it was good it was the end of the season, and he would have plenty of time to consider his words, thoughts, and feelings if there were questions later.

After the others left, he wanted to spend time with Austen and David to ask what they thought of the program. The little boy was still keyed up from seeing himself. And disregarding the fact he had purposely stayed away from Austen after seeing what everyone who watched would see, he needed to be close to her. He remembered that kiss after they stopped on the highway and just as she did, he wanted to experience it again.

He settled for taking her hand, kissing it, then wrapped her in his arms. She returned the embrace and laid her head on his shoulder, wanting to stay there.

Since the next day was Sunday, Austen wondered if they would be attending church services again. She wanted to, and finally worked up enough courage to ask Mark. Though she and David could go on their own, she wanted to be with him.

He gave her what might be considered a loving look and asked, "Do you want to?"

"I wouldn't have asked unless I did."

"Okay, same schedule as last Sunday. I'll be ready to leave at eight thirty." She felt it might be the last opportunity to fill herself with some quiet serenity. She hoped it would do the same thing for Mark.

After the services, they came directly home with nothing said about a meal. Thankfully, bless Kate, she called to invite them for lunch. Austen and David accepted, but no one seemed to know where Mark had gone.

Sad as she was about what was happening to them, she prayed for peace in his heart. How she wished there were something she could say or do to make a difference for him, but she had tried all she knew how to.

That afternoon, she took the opportunity to try to prepare David for their leaving, or at least begin to.

"David, do you remember the long ride when we drove from home to get here?"

She could see he was trying to, but young as he was, maybe he didn't. He had slept a lot and they had stopped often.

He finally said, "I don't know."

"We stayed with Grandpa and Grandma a few days before we started the trip."

With a smile, he said, "We had fun."

"We left very early in the morning; it was still dark, and Grandpa carried you to the car. We drove a long time and a long way to get here, where we met Kate and Bill and Mark."

At the mention of Mark, his sweet smile spread across his face.

"I love him."

"Yes, now we will have to leave here to drive the other way, to go back to Grandpa and Grandma."

"Will Mark go with us?

"No, he lives here."

"We live here."

"Yes, for now; but it's his forever home; we're just here for a little while."

How hard it was trying to explain to him. "We'll be here a few more days; then we have to go."

"But we love him, Mommie Mark will miss us if we go. He loves us. Why can't we stay here?"

She decided that was enough for now. He probably wouldn't ever understand and wouldn't grasp it until they were in the car driving away.

She had received a text from Jerilyn to let her know they arrived home safely and to ask if she had seen Josh lately. Austen hoped their courtship, or relationship, or whatever it might be, would be less complicated than hers and Mark's.

As part of her preparation for leaving in a few days, she asked Bill if he would take her car to be serviced, wanting to be sure there would be no problems on that long drive. Like David, she had come to feel like TrailWays and Mark were home. The trip would be just as hard for her as for him.

The last days of August were slow; many kids had gone back to school, and parents were back to work after vacations. At TrailWays, they were already preparing for the fall and winter hiatus and next spring's events.

Then came the day for the last church service of the summer at TrailWays, when she planned to wear the dress she had made. It was fashioned as a Sunday-best dress appropriate to the 1840s, when people were heading toward Oregon. She had engrossed herself in the history of the pioneers, read their diaries, studied pictures illustrating the time, and, as much as possible, relived their experience on the trail. With this dress, she almost felt she had been transported back to that time.

Few dressed up for the services, but this was the last one of the summer, and the last for her. She planned to leave the dress with Kate for someone to wear in following years. She would have enough memories of the summer without that particular reminder.

Even David seemed to sense a difference and told her, "Mommie, you look just like those old womans in the pictures."

She knew what he meant, even though his words did tend to bring her back down to earth. He couldn't quite comprehend that the pictures that hung on the walls here and throughout the buildings of TrailWays were old, depicting another time, but the people pictured were not necessarily old.

Since she was wearing her special dress, she had asked Kate and Bill for a ride and didn't want to keep them waiting. But as she and David were leaving their wing of the house and entered the main living area, Mark was standing with his back to them, blocking the outside door, and Austen heard him telling someone to go on, that he would take care of it.

Just as always, her heart speeded up as soon as she saw him; but what was he doing here? He usually went early to prepare the site, and since their relationship had been so strained recently, she expected he would have made sure he was gone before she headed that way.

There was no way she could get through the door with him standing there, and it didn't look like he was planning on leaving just yet. She was debating what to do when David whooped, "Mark! Are you going with us today? See Mommie's new dress? She made it on Kate's machine." Then he repeated to Mark his belief that "she looks like those old peoples on the wall."

At the first sound of David's voice, the man had turned around and that infuriating grin appeared on his face at the little boy's last words. His eyes went around the room, looking at the pictures of the pioneers which graced the walls.

"You're right, cowboy, she looks just like those old peoples."

Then, surveying himself, he added, "Looks like I should have dressed up for the occasion."

As far as Austen was concerned, her heart couldn't have stood it if he dressed any differently than his regular western shirts and tight jeans. He didn't seem inclined to move from the doorway, so, finally finding her voice, she told him, "Kate and Bill are waiting for us and we're already late, so may we please pass?"

"Wrong."

"What do you mean, wrong?"

"They're already gone."

"But they can't be! I know we're a little late, but they wouldn't have gone without us."

"I told them to go on. I'm taking you."

So though she had not expected it, she was going to have this one more day with him. When they reached the site, he found seats allowing the three of them to sit together.

Twenty Two

Activities for Labor Day would be much as they were for the Fourth of July, except for the fireworks. She had checked with Bill and Kate previously, as she wanted to be prepared. But it felt like she was preparing for a funeral.

David, as usual, was with Mark and she left him alone; it would be his last day with the man he loved so much. She was avoiding him, withdrawing into herself, trying not to feel, knowing she would be leaving the next day.

After her last short trek, she mingled through the crowd where Josh joined her. She was visiting and telling some people goodbye.

He asked, "Have you heard from Jerilyn?"

She came back with a smile, "Have you?"

"We've kept in touch since she was here," then, sighing, he added, "There sure are a lot of miles between here and there."

"How I know that—not just miles, but hours. Though I suppose flying would reduce that."

"So has school started yet?"

"We had orientation last week. Real classes start tomorrow. Have to be there at seven a.m."

"You keep looking around for someone or something special?"

"Yeah, Mark."

"I think he left. David was with him; then the next thing I knew, Bill had him. Did you need him for something?"

"No, I was remembering that day in town when we were officially introduced. I was probably flirting with you, or trying to. He didn't say anything, but looked like he could take off my head. Today, he might actually do that."

"Probably not."

"I've seen the way he looks at you, and no one could miss it if they saw that TV broadcast."

That brought tears to her eyes as she was remembering that day she and Mark had driven to the station to review the film, and then the ride home.

Josh asked, "What did I say?"

Austen told him, "No matter how he looks at me or what you think you know, Mark and I are never going to be together. He's pretty much made it clear he won't marry again. But knowing that didn't keep me from falling in love with him.

"There won't be any happily ever after for me."

Josh put his arms around her, tentatively still watching in case Mark was there.

Pulling back, Austen told him, "Thanks; sorry for unloading on you."

"So what's next for you?"

"David and I are leaving tomorrow; not quite sure what time yet; probably won't drive straight through. I do remember those many miles." She added, "So glad I got to know you. Maybe I'll see you again?"

Smiling, Josh said, "Yeah, maybe."

After hearing Austen's tale, Josh texted Jerilyn to tell her about Mark's actions and how Austen had responded. Then he told her, "Let's not ever act like that." Seemingly, he was looking toward a long relationship.

The last time she saw David, he was still with Bill. Mark had disappeared. Would he be at the house tonight, or before she left the next day? Had she already seen him for the last time, and he hadn't even said goodbye?

Kate had told her to plan to come to her house for supper and asked her about breakfast the next day.

Austen told her, "I'll think about it. May not let you know 'til morning, though."

The afternoon and early evening seemed to drag, but at the same time, she didn't want the time to pass. She felt she was shriveling up inside. Why did Mark have to be such a coward? Why did she have to fall in love with him? Why had no one been able to convince him he still had a right to love? She knew she hadn't misinterpreted the fact that he loved her; there were too many clues, and other actions that were so much more than clues.

Bill brought David to her and said, "Why don't you call it a day?"

He couldn't miss the sadness in her eyes, and gave her a hug. He had an idea of what she was feeling, and no one could do anything about it.

She and David went by the house before going to the Pearsons' for supper. She wanted to take the dress to Kate, and this would be a good time to do that. There was no evidence that Mark had been there since he left that morning—if he had been there even then. She had hoped to have at least one more hour with him, and thought about texting him, but decided against it. What would she say?

She moved through the evening in a daze, even while at the Pearsons'. David was tired from his day and fell asleep early. She was more exhausted from heartbreak than fatigue, but having no reason to stay up, she was in bed early too, sleeping restlessly through the night. If there were dreams, she didn't remember.

She called Bill to ask if he could come to get David for breakfast.

"I want to stay here for awhile longer to make sure everything is okay." She didn't want Mark to remember her in any negative way. "Have you seen or heard from Mark since yesterday?"

"Sorry, no."

Austen told him, "I'm not sure he's been home. I may knock on his door later. Maybe he's here and still sleeping." Though she was sure that wasn't the case.

He knew she was planning to leave, so her departure must not mean anything to him. Maybe it was a relief she wouldn't be around any longer. In the future, he would probably check out the help a little more thoroughly before hiring by mail.

She had already gathered hers and David's things and began to load them into the car; and so she wouldn't forget, she also left her purse with her phone in it.

As she was completing her inspection, she found something that made her feel even worse, if that was possible. She didn't know when he could have done it, but she found an envelope on the table holding a check and a note.

The note only said, "Thank you for the summer. Be careful on the way home. Mark." No Mrs. Wiley, no "love." Nothing to indicate he even felt a friendship for her, let alone the love she knew he had, as did everyone else who knew him.

Rashly she tore the check, the note, and the envelope into as many pieces as she could. She had already gathered pen and paper to write him a note, and she vowed to do that anyway, spilling out all her feelings.

~

He had said nothing to Josh about going to his house, but there he was at midnight. Where had he been before? Everyone was looking for him. He had stopped by his house when he was sure Austen and David were asleep to leave a check and short note for her. He wasn't actually sure where he was going after that; he just wanted to be away.

His knock woke up Josh. "Can I stay here until Austen leaves?"

Josh threw a sheet and pillow toward him, then said, "I'll talk to you in the morning."

Josh slept; Mark didn't.

Josh arose at six o'clock and told Mark he had to be at school in an hour and wanted to have some breakfast. Then he began his lecture.

"I've watched you all summer; you changed from a grouch to a man glowing with love. You're so much in love with Austen, it's been almost magic being around you. And she's been the same. Wake up; don't throw away that gift."

Mark replied, "But you were with me before; don't you remember how it was—how I was?"

Josh agreed, saying, "I was, and it was nothing like this. You were shocked and upset and hurt, but you were more mad than anything else, and mad at yourself, if you're truthful.

"You probably loved Tricia; but it was nothing compared to how you feel about Austen; you know that. Anyone who watched that TV broadcast knows it. You couldn't even bear to watch.

"I remember the time this summer when I first 'officially' met her and started to flirt—like I do. I thought you were going to take my head off; but you didn't say a thing."

"If you let her go, I don't think you'll be able to function, and I know you'll never get over it. The business will probably deteriorate. You've been so dysfunctional the last two weeks I don't think you even know it; and, you've reverted to what you were before she came.

"The last few days—or weeks—you have avoided her as much as you could, so you don't have any idea that she is fading away. We're all worried about her and David having to drive back to Kansas. It's like she's lost, and lost her heart at the same time."

Josh then received a text from Bill, asking, "Do you know where Mark is?" He replied, "He's here."

"You still have time to stop her. If you don't, I'm going to call you stupid every day for the rest of your life. And I don't have any more time. I'm due at school in less than an hour, and I'm not ready.

"If you want to save her life and yours, you've got to go—stop her—finally tell her in words how you feel. And ask her to forgive you."

~

Austen was hurt almost beyond bearing with the note he had left. And it came out in the one she left for him.

Dear Mr. Thomas,

I think I fell in love with you that first day we met—even though there was tension between us from the beginning.

We had almost-kisses, and more, immediately, as if our hearts were longing to feel love again. Though we both fought those feelings, I think you did more than I.

I didn't know why that was for a long time—then I learned the person you loved and had married didn't come home one day. I can only imagine how that hurt, and how you probably questioned your judgment.

Still, just as I fell in love with you, I believe you fell in love with me. There have been too many times when I've seen it in your eyes, and felt it finally in those wonderful kisses you gave me.

You began to give contrary actions—as if you wanted me to be with you, and at the same time not saying or doing anything to keep me here—pushing and pulling.

And me—I was hurt—my heart broken anew every day. Though you apologized for some of those hurts, there were many you didn't even seem aware of.

All the way up to today, the day I was originally to start my trip back home. But I want this to be my home—with you. You chose not to be here—because you couldn't bear to watch me leave? Where are you? David and I have our things packed in the car, ready to go. He has hardly stopped crying. Do you know how much he loves you? You have been so good to him and for him, and I am grateful for that. I will have to be careful driving, as I'll be crying all the way.

When I left Kansas to come here, I thought Mark Thomas might be old and fat, bald and ugly. I wish you had been; I wouldn't feel this way.

I won't come back. If you want me, you'll have to come for me.

I will love you forever.

Mrs. Wiley

She placed the letter on the table, sprinkled it with the torn-up note and check, and anchored it with a salt shaker.

After composing herself, she knocked on his door, opened it, and went in, hoping that for just awhile she could feel close to him once more. She was prompted to open his closet, wondering what he would do or say; would he know if she took one of his western shirts? Unable to help herself, she removed one from its hanger and began sobbing, placed it against her eyes, and fell onto his bed face-down.

Her mother had been trying to reach her, but since her phone was in her purse in the car, she didn't know. Mrs. Morgan finally called Kate to find out whether her daughter and grandson had started on their way.

At the same time, Bill was trying to call Mark to no avail because his phone was in his pickup.

Mark had finally heard what Josh was telling him and drove home as fast as he could. He parked beside Austen's car, glad to see it was still there, and went inside. First thing he saw was the letter she had left, and what was left of his note and check. He picked it up and read it, crying and laughing at the same time, then went looking for her.

His heart lurched when he saw her on his bed; he strode to her and pulled her into his arms, saying, "Your fat, bald, ugly old man is here." Then he drew her closer and gave her one of those kisses that filled her being. As he wrapped his arms around her, she noticed the dark stubble on his chin, recalling that first meeting when it had first drawn her attention.

When he briefly removed his lips from hers, she heard, "pesky mosquito." She would have to ask him about that sometime.

Since Bill was unsuccessful in reaching Mark, and Austen hadn't appeared at their house, he drove down to Mark's and saw both vehicles. Debating with himself whether to enter, he finally knocked on the door, and when there was no answer, went on in. The couple was wrapped up in each other and weren't aware of his presence. When he saw them, a smile spread across his face; he quietly let himself out, then drove home and told Kate, "Call Mrs. Morgan and tell her Austen won't be coming home."

Twenty Three

She had slept fitfully the night before; he not at all. As they lay together savoring their new closeness, both dropped off to sleep wrapped in each other's arms. But just before sleep overtook her, she heard, "I love you."

Since both their phones were still in their vehicles, there would be no interruptions.

When Bill got back to his house, he told David that his mommie and Mark were at home. "They're tired, so they may take a nap, but you don't have to leave after all, you're going to stay at Mark's house."

David told him, "I wanta see Mommie and Mark."

Bill tried to call them, not knowing their phones were in their vehicles. As he had done earlier, he knocked on the door when he got back there—and still no answer. He and David went in anyway.

Mark and Austen were still sleeping, tangled together on the bed. David ran in, jumping on top of them. Awake immediately, Mark smiled and asked, "Is it okay for me to marry your mommie?"

David didn't know what that meant, but nodded his head anyway. It was then Bill told them, "Your phones must be somewhere else because no one can get in touch with you."

It took a while for them to realize where their phones were. Mark said, "I'll get them. I'm hungry, need to see what we have to make breakfast, or brunch, maybe lunch."

He got up after giving Austen a kiss on the lips. Bill noticed how happy and exuberant and free he was, thinking, it's about time. She couldn't hide her happiness, but blushed thinking about Bill standing there watching, though there was nothing improper to see. They were both fully dressed and not even under the covers.

As she got up, she said, "I need to contact my mother. She's probably frantic."

Bill told her, "No worries. Kate told her you wouldn't be coming home."

She wondered how they had known, but maybe it was better if she didn't.

When Mark came back with their phones, he told her, "There are things I want to say to you, but guess we'll have to wait awhile since David is dancing around both of us." He kissed her again.

Going to the kitchen, he began checking the refrigerator and cabinets for something to prepare a meal, with David and Austen right beside him.

Bill knew Josh would be in the classroom, but was probably wondering what had happened with Mark, so he texted to let him know all was well.

Austen was so filled with love, she was almost fearful after the summer of ups and downs with Mark. Did she dare believe the new status was real? She finally felt free to express her feelings, to touch, to hug, to kiss, to open herself, to not feel that she needed to hold back.

She loved getting the quick, sweet, affectionate, spontaneous kisses as much as she did the deeper ones which created such longing. So what would happen, and when? He had asked David if he could marry his mommie; but hadn't asked her. For how long would she be in his house?—so close to him—and hopefully his kisses, yet still no permanent commitment.

When would she have confidence in the future and experience no more uncertainties?

She remembered that he had said he had things to tell her. What did that mean? After the summer, she found she was impatient.

Mark must have really been hungry, since he created a meal of scrambled eggs, bacon, hash browns, toast with jelly and orange marmalade, fruit, and juice. And of course, the almost requisite coffee. But perhaps it was a hunger for more than food.

Austen's mother called while they were eating, wanting more complete information than Kate had given her. Austen gave her a brief synopsis of everything, including the fact that Mark had asked David if he could marry his mommie.

Immediately she was asked, "When and where will you have the wedding? Will it be a small one, or several attendants?"

Austen had moved from the table so she could talk more freely, then told her mother, "He didn't ask me, Mom. I'll let you know if you need to plan a trip. I will tell you, I no longer have doubts about his love for me. He even said it. And, Mom, I feel so loved and so much in love I can hardly think."

Mark came up behind her while she was still talking to her mother, and began nuzzling her neck.

Saying, "I'll talk to you later, Mom," she ended the call, then turned in his arms for one of those kisses she was almost getting used to.

"Why did I fight this all summer?" Mark asked. "I'm sorry."

His arms around her, he rested his head on hers, and together they rocked back and forth.

At the end of the day, with David asleep and in bed, Mark led her to the couch, sat down, and pulled her onto his lap. "I told you there were things I wanted to say to you. Believe it or not, I first knew I loved you when you were standing outside your cabin door with the morning sun making a halo out of that unruly hair of yours. I only said you should whack it off because I didn't like the way it made me feel. Actually think I didn't want to feel; I had been determined to never get mixed up with a woman ever again; then, there you stood."

Tightening his arms, he told her, "It took all my resistance not to grab you and carry you to my bed right then. You can't imagine all the frustration I've gone through all these weeks, watching you, wanting to help you, even doing it for you. In those first days, I was looking for all the wrong things you did. How could I possibly be in love with a woman so inept at everything that's been important to me the last few years? But you persisted, refusing to give up. I love your determination; your stubbornness; your ability to prevail whatever the circumstances; your ability to make the best of any situation, and to make others feel good about themselves."

"So I wasted the summer, except for those rare special times."

She turned to kiss him, then moved from his lap to sit beside him. He wrapped his arms around her and pulled her back against him.

"I think you know my frustrations; actually I wanted to hate you, but David had taken to you right away, and you seemed to return that caring. I did want to find something to please you, and although I was useless at first with all the trail things, I loved it anyway. Actually, until the last few weeks, I dreaded for the first of September to arrive, when it would all be over and I would have to leave."

"I heard what you told your mother," he said. Then he moved from behind her; got down on one knee, and asked, "Will you marry me, Mrs. Wiley?"

"Yes, yes, yes, Mr. Thomas."

Almost soberly, he said, "I'll be glad when you're Mrs. Thomas."

Then there was a special kiss to seal the promise.

"Sorry, guess you know I wasn't expecting this; I haven't been to the jewelers, so no ring. We'll go tomorrow and pick out rings together."

"We've wasted all summer; maybe I should say I've wasted all summer. I don't want to wait any longer. Anyway, if it's okay with you, I want to get married as soon as your folks can arrange to be here. Guess I need to let my parents know too."

"I'm ok with that; but there are things we need to decide. Remember Patsy wanted to be in our wedding when we got married? Maybe you didn't hear that?"

"Yes, I did, just wanted to ignore it."

"And I would like to have a special dress. I don't even know where to look for one. And David will need something. Since it's going to be in such a short time, some people might not be able to get time off to come to the wedding, let alone have the responsibility of being an attendant. How about just having Patsy as flower girl, David as ring bearer, and you and me?"

"You've been thinking about this."

"Of course. I kept dreaming and hoping. Even when I was packing and raiding your closet."

"What happened to that shirt, anyway?"

"It's in my room; I'm going to sleep in it."

"I like that; if I can't be there, guess that's the next best thing. I'll think about its arms wrapped around you.

"Can we at least choose a date—long enough away that we can get everything done that needs to be, and contact all the people we need to—but still not too long?"

"I bet you have an idea of when?"

"Yesterday," Mark told her.

Austin responded with "I wish that could have happened; but now it's yesterday's tomorrow, so we missed that date."

"How do you feel about the first Saturday in October? It's too long for me, but I know these things take time."

"We'll make it work. That's about four weeks."

Her head was swimming as she began thinking about all the details. She needed to make a list, starting with contacting everyone, including the Wileys, Don's parents.

She called her mother the next morning. "Mom, you will probably have to stay at a motel. I don't know where Mark's parents will stay, or his brother and his family, or Linda, if she comes. No idea whether any of my group from church will plan to come. As you know so well, to drive that distance is almost an ordeal; then to turn around in a day or two and go the other way. I'm going to send a letter to the Wileys. It's going to be hard, and I can only imagine how they will feel. But maybe they'll decide to come. I don't know when we'll have a chance to go back there, though I will want to go through my things in storage sometime and decide what to keep."

She left it to Mark to notify his family, including asking Patsy if she would like to be flower girl. "Austen said she needs your size so she can get a special dress for you."

Texts were sent to friends, hers and his, with the expectation they would soon get texts in return, many expressing surprise.

They decided to take David with them later that morning as they drove to see a jeweler in Scottsbluff, choosing one Mark was familiar with. She didn't want to ask if it was where he had bought the ones for his marriage to Tricia. It had been enough years that hopefully they wouldn't remember if that were the case.

The man brought out several trays of rings appropriate for engagements and weddings. As they selected different rings to examine and try on, the jeweler kept glancing from one to the other, trying to be surreptitious. Austen wondered if he might have remembered a previous time when Mark was choosing rings.

Then he exclaimed, "I knew you looked familiar."

At those words, Austen wanted to shrink into herself. Then she heard, "You're that guy from TrailWays, and you're beautiful Austen! Congratulations. Thanks for coming here; I appreciate your business."

"And who is this young man with you?"

"I'm Cowboy," David said, drawing a smile from the man.

Mark simply told him, "This is David, a good friend of mine." Then hugging him, drew him onto his lap.

They agreed on a set of rings, engagement, and the two wedding bands, which required little adjustment. The jeweler told them they should be ready in just a few days.

When they left the store, they drove around and Mark pointed out a shop that sold wedding gowns as well as any other dresses for a wedding, even for flower girls.

He parked and they got out so she could look around to see if there was anything she felt drawn to.

He suggested, "Maybe you and Kate can come shopping? I think I want to be surprised and not see you in your dress until you walk down the aisle."

She hadn't noticed 'til then that Lissa Courtney's shop was nearby. Seeing the distress on her face, Mark put his arm around her and said, "I never had any feelings for her; never will. And when you live here, you will come to Scottsbluff regularly, and there's always the possibility you might run into her. Just know I love you. And I'm pretty sure she knows it too." Then he kissed her.

Neither had seen Lissa looking through the window of her shop, with a sad look on her face.

They found a place to eat pizza, then drove home. Austen called Kate later to make plans to go shopping in a couple of days. She still needed Patsy's dress size, so she called and talked to Matt's wife Peggy, who told her Patsy was so excited to be in the wedding. She had hardly stopped talking about her and David since she got back home.

Mark took responsibility for talking with the pastor and reserving the church, plus talking to Barry about catering, although they still needed to find a venue for the reception. The band would provide the music for both.

Jerilyn texted Austen, telling her she was so happy for her and that she and Josh had talked about the wedding. He wanted her to come, and she was thinking of taking a day off so she could attend. Josh had an extra room and she would probably stay there.

The weeks flew by, though not to Mark. He felt each day passed at a snail's pace, and asked himself constantly why he had wasted a summer. But finally the day of the rehearsal arrived. All the people who loved them had worked together to get everything ready.

Despite the distance for many of those who came, there would be a full church, including David's Wiley grandparents. There was a brief moment of awkwardness when they met, but they were very cordial to Mark, as he was to them.

With so few attendants, the rehearsal took very little time. Mark's father asked David if he was excited that his mommie was going to marry Mark. He looked confused and said, "I don't know. What does that mean?"

Before anyone else could say anything, Patsy told him, "It means they can sleep in the same bed." And all the adults were glad to have the question answered in such a simple way. They would have made it so complicated.

Then it was finally that wonderful special day. Mark's parents were taking care of David at his house, getting him dressed in his wedding clothes as he called them. Mark almost needed help himself, he was so nervous. He was wearing a blue western-cut suit that had been custom made for him. A bolo with a silver slide matching his belt buckle was at the neck of his white western shirt. Even his boots had silver tips.

Austen's parents were with her at the Pearsons', where she was getting dressed with her mother's help. Her lace appliqué dress had long sleeves and was low in the back with a chapel train. The veil was also of lace appliqué. Her mother thought she had never looked more beautiful.

Kate and Bill were already at the church, overseeing much of the preparation. They had made sure the building was decorated and that the band was in place. They had even arranged for a photographer.

The florist from Plattsford had prepared the bridal bouquet of red and yellow roses, the pillow for the rings, and the basket of petals for the flower girl, as well as the corsages for parents and the wedding party. She was positioned in the foyer, where she could make sure each of them received the correct one, and her assistant helped pin them on.

Mark was standing nervously at the altar, and when he felt he could no longer stand the wait, the back door opened, and there stood Austen with her parents. From then on, to him she was the only person in the building, more beautiful than he remembered.

The band had been playing for several minutes. When the music changed to "Here Comes the Bride," Patsy started down the aisle, dropping the red and yellow rose petals, with David behind holding the pillow with the rings very carefully. Then Austen, carrying her bouquet, started down the aisle toward him, a parent on each side.

When she reached Mark, her parents gave her to him, and then she passed the bouquet to her mother.

Afterwards, neither remembered much of the service; they were so absorbed in each other. The pastor had to remind them twice about the rings; Mark's hand actually shook as he placed the wedding ring on her finger. David had wanted to be with them and climbed up the few steps to stand with the couple. No one made a move to change that; they looked like a family being merged together.

Austen's parents sat with the Wileys. It was a poignant picture for them. They were happy that Austen had found a man that loved her so much, and from the first time they had met had become a father figure for David. They were sad that David never had the opportunity to know his own father, but Mark would be a good one.

Austen and Mark enjoyed the reception and were grateful for all those who had helped put it together; many of the details they had not thought of. It was so good to mingle with the guests and receive their love and congratulations. They were people who had watched the two and were glad there had been a happy ending to the summer.

Little had been said about a possible honeymoon, though Hawaii had been mentioned. Then, thinking of David, they decided to forego one, at least for now. The little boy was still somewhat confused about all that had happened the last few weeks and they didn't want to create a new concern for him if they left for a week.

Knowing that, both sets of his grandparents, plus Mark's parents and Kate and Bill, decided to each take turns keeping David for a night, making it possible for him to see his mommie and Mark a few hours each day. This was certainly not customary, but maybe they could call it a TrailWays Honeymoon. Mark and Austen accepted it as a wonderful suggestion.

During the first dance, Mark told her, "I'm looking forward to our honeymoon, Mrs. Thomas."

"Me too, Mr. Thomas."

They looked around to see where David was, and Mark called, "Hey, cowboy, come join us."

He ran to them and Mark picked him up so the three could finish the dance together.

One Year Later

As they looked back on the past year, it was still hard for Mark and Austen to believe they were so blessed. Even TrailWays had become a more popular destination the past summer, with new events added.

And there was baby Morgan, who had been given her mother's maiden name, just as Austen had been. David adored his baby sister. He had always thought Mark was his, and now, so was she. He even called her "My Morgan." He loved her babbling and spent much time trying to make her smile.

Kate called it God's mysterious way—it was just as she had thought that first day, remembering how their life together had started—contentious, but with love already weaving into their consciousness.

Acknowledgements

Special thanks to Leslie Largent, who first urged me to finish a book I had started years ago, then continually inspired me as I made progress.

And thank you to Patricia Burton, who supported, encouraged, and motivated me through the entire process.